Faith Spi

Aria Towards Destruction

Also by Vivienne Saint Louis

The Sister's Affinity
Faith Spiritwolfe Pain and Knowledge
Faith Spiritwolfe - Aria Towards Destruction

Standalone
Dreaming Awake - Selected Poetry and Prose

Watch for more at https://www.vivisaint.weebly.com.

Table of Contents

Vivienne Saint Louis

Faith Spiritwolfe
Aria Towards Destruction

This Edition Published 2020

Imprint: Independently Published

Printed in the United States of America

Text © 2019 Vanessa Michelle Roberson

Vivienne Saint Louis

vivisaint.weebly.com

Faith Spiritwolfe Books
The Sisters Affinity Book 1
Pain and Knowledge
The Sisters Affinity Book 2
Aria Towards Destruction2
The Sisters Affinity Book 3

Part One
Aria

I dedicate this book to Han Seungwoo of VICTON who never gave up on his dreams and endured various obstacles to reach his goals. Through his persistence, I was inspired to not give on my dreams as well. Han Seungwoo, I celebrate your life and your beautiful music as it helped me complete this book. Your kindness, selflessness, perseverance, and your incredible smile kept me going when I was at my lowest. You became my 'Light' and I will forever be grateful to you.

Let's walk down the flowery path together.

Forever Your ALICE

1

Subterfuge

"To create chaos, one has to first create a sense of peace so when all hell breaks loose, people will do anything to get things back to normal." –

Anonymous

Faith Spiritwolfe had many reasons to dread her 17th birthday. One, she was no longer on speaking terms with the person she thought was her father. Two, she was still uncomfortable around the people she thought were her relatives. And three, a demon Queen was trying to recruit her because she was the half demon daughter of her husband who could start fires, see ghost, and transform into a panther. *'What's to celebrate?'* she thought while sitting at the white marbled desk in her boyfriend Lex's house. She spent most of her free time there, even when he was not home.

Faith's legal home and address was still with the Andrews in their West Side townhouse, no matter how little time she spent there. "It's not a home, it's a facsimile," she muttered with a flip of her spiral locks.

"What is?" came the sultry voice of her platinum haired boyfriend, though a boy was not what she would call him. 'What do you call an immortal being with supernatural powers who stopped aging long ago? He explained to her that in his world, the magical realm of Dorcela, he was still an adolescent like her.'

Lex leaned over the desk and planted a warm kiss on Faith's cheek. He lingered close to her ear causing her to shiver with delight. His kisses had an effect of drawing her negative thoughts away but not this time.

"The Andrews home is not a home. It's a bad joke," she said bitingly, her eyes on the blank sheet of paper in front of her that should be her completed homework.

"Blood alone doesn't define family Faith," said Lex while slipping his arms around her shoulders, his lips still at her ear. "Look at my family, full of back stabbers and plotters and they are my flesh and blood. Devonte still considers you his cousin and nothing will turn him from that notion. Do you want your relationship with him to alter?"

"I...," Faith thought about Dev's enigmatic smile and his playful nature and she knew she wouldn't want to do without them for long. Devonte was the only person who didn't treat her differently after finding out who her real father was. He was more shocked to hear that his mother had their sealed their powers when they left Dorcela to raise Faith in order to keep Nemfora off their radar. It worked for a while but moving to New York three months ago, exposed them all to the magical dangers they thought they had left behind.

"It would be worth celebrating your birthday to see the people who truly care about you," said Lex, tightening his hold on her.

"How did you know I was worried about celebrating my birthday?"

"It's the only thing you wrote on your paper."

True enough, Faith had absentmindedly scribbled the words 'my birthday' in the corner of her homework. She hastily erased it and spun around in her chair so that she was facing Lex. His usually tidy hair was tousled and damp from a recent shower. Faith bit her lower lip as she fought against a need she scarcely knew she had. His white shirt clung to the water droplets left on his skin leaving little to the imagination. Possibly sensing her eyeing, him like a steak, he spun her back towards the desk.

"Finish your work while I get changed into dry clothes," he said, lightly ruffling her hair. Faith swatted his hand away and he disappeared out the study to his bedroom. Faith plunged straight in with her homework, liking how the busy work kept her mind off her troubles. She was well into her AP Physics homework when her navy-blue phone started buzzing beside the fat book she was perusing.

A familiar anxiety caused her heart to race but then she quelled it when she saw the name 'Saoirse' flash on the tiny screen. It was a text message with a number of smiling and frowning little pictures illustrating what she texted.

Hey Faith, missed you at lunch today. :(

Saw you eating with 'them' >>

I know you have to keep up appearances with those people but do not forget who your friends are hun <3

See you at dinner tonight yeah? o.o

"Keeping up appearances," said Faith aloud. Her new lunch table was a lot like work so keeping up appearances was the right way to describe it. She and Lex came up with a way for them to be seen together without harming either one of their causes, but it meant Faith had to see less of her actual friends. Saoirse knew her reason was dire, but it did not stop her from complaining about not seeing her. Faith had a lot more on her plate than just her New York family drama. She was the love child of a human energy sucking demon who was married to the Queen of the demon race known as Demimages. His wife, Nemfora had a number of children but one in particular hated Faith from the moment she knew she was conceived, her half-sister Flammare.

Luckily, Faith was no pushover, she had inherited powers from both of her parents, flame from her father Damiel and shapeshifting from her mother Chryselda. Although technically this made Faith a half Demimage, she was considered a Light Mage, a being of peace. And that is what Faith wanted, peace and freedom. But there was another desire deep inside her, a desire that she could not fight no matter how hard she tried. She wanted to meet her birth father Damiel. The man who had seduced her mother into cheating on the man Faith thought was her father.

It was that desire that changed her current lunch time arrangements at her school Alexander Prep where a number of Nemfora's children attended. She thought getting close to her half siblings would help her achieve one of her goals. It had the added bonus of being where Lex also ate lunch for he was a spy among Nemfora's Demimages and wanted nothing more but to bring her down.

Saoirse knew most of this of course but it did not stop her wanting to see her friend. Faith texted what she thought was a heartfelt message to her oldest and closets friend and hoped it would be enough to quell her frustration at least for a little while.

Heya Soar

Sorry I had to ditch you at lunch today.

I promise to make it up to you tonight at dinner.

I'm bringing dessert.

It's just I can't be seen being all buddy buddy with Affinity members right now.

It would set me back weeks. Please try and understand.

Lots of Love

Faith

She re-read it twice before sending it. 'That should do the trick,' she thought, and her eyes lingered over the word "Affinity." Another complication. The Sisters Affinity was a group she briefly was a part of but now she wanted nothing to do with them. They like her wanted to bring Nemfora and her demons down, but they had vastly different ideas about how to accomplish it.

As if she did not have enough on her plate, the group of Light Mages harbored a closet Demimage. The once Second-In-Command leader of the Affinity, Rin blamed Faith's mother and subsequently Faith herself for inadvertently causing her mother's death. Nemfora found out about Damiel's infidelity and retaliated by killing all the members of the Sister's Affinity when they gave birth. Rin revenged herself upon Faith. Faith was strong enough to fight her off and caused the traitor to flee but according to Lex, she was not gone forever.

The Affinity kept too much about her past from her and was tainted in her mind. She parted ways with the group with Saoirse still a member and decided to fight Nemfora on her own as naive as it sounded but with Lex by her side she did not think it was impossible.

Faith went back to her homework on Subatomic Particles and waited for Saoirse to reply. 10 minutes inched by painfully slow before her phone buzzed again with a noticeably short text message.

Bring pie.

Lex did not return to the study until an hour after he had exited the room. This time he was fully dressed in a white tunic and maroon pants tucked into a pair of black boots. Faith chuckled to herself thinking he looked like a pirate from a theme park. All he was missing was a cutlass and bad teeth.

"What's with the that getup?"

"Gotta see Her Highness this evening. She has a distain for mortal clothing," said Lex as he gracefully tied his shoulder length locks into a ponytail at the base of his head. At this Faith's expression turned from playful to curiosity with just a hint of envy.

"You're going to see Nemfora? I wish you could take me with you."

Lex paused his grooming to stare at his girlfriend who peered wide eyed and expectantly up at him. Sensing she had him where she wanted him, Faith leapt out of her chair like a feline and slithered close to him, her fingers playing on the buttons of his pants and she felt him tense up.

"Can't I go with you?" she begged in a low voice; her lips were just inches from his. She could see them parting ever so slightly and smell his minty fresh breath.

"Faith," he said warningly, tilting his head down in disapproval. "It's too soon, you know it. We have to play it cool yeah. Both of our lives are at stake here. She can't ever find out who I really am." Faith wasn't the only one keeping up appearances, Lex was deep undercover in Nemfora's group as the demon Pride Leafander, a facade Faith voluntarily helped to keep up. The platinum blond Alexei Cloud Sky she saw was not what the demons saw when they laid eyes on him. Faith had no idea what Pride looked like and sometimes, especially when he kissed her in public, she did wonder.

"I know," Faith muttered, her eyes drooping. "It's just the last time she had you on assignment, you were gone a week. I spent the night at the Andrews house dogging questions from Letitia and Dev." Devonte's mother Letitia accepted that Faith still felt uncomfortable around her knowing she wasn't really her niece but whenever she was home, she would bombard her with questions about her current life, a current life that was full of secrecy and untold nights spent at Lex's and not Saoirse's.

"It was rough being away from you too," said Lex, pulling Faith's hand to his lips and kissing her fingers, causing Faith's lips to spread into a satisfied smile. "A week of doing Nemfora's bidding...unspeakable horrors I never want you exposed to."

"I will have to be exposed to them eventually won't I if our plan succeeds?" Faith argued not appreciating being treated like someone who needed to be shielded from the truth of his work for Nemfora.

"Yes, eventually. Too fast and she will become suspicious. Nemfora is not to be taken lightly. Not ever. You know what she is capable of."

Faith frowned at the subtle mention of her mother's murder at Nemfora's hands. Sure, it was the reality of what they were facing but Faith was not going to back down. She knew what she wanted and like her mother before her, she was going to do whatever it took to accomplish it.

"Then go but come back to me...soon."

Lex dropped Faith's hand and pulled her close then his soft full lips were on hers. His kiss was like a promise. Sweet, lingering and left her hungry for more. He ended the kiss with a light caress of her face then he pulled away from her and dissolved into wisps of smoke that floated out the open window and out of sight.

2

The New Normal

"I think I am falling in love." - Anonymous

It did not take long for Faith to learn the new status quo at school. Cyphren and his friends were popular, so people sat around their table at every break time. The only time it was not crowded was when students were supposed to be in class and the hall monitors would stalk around it to make sure it stayed empty. Their table was the closest to the back of the room so people did whatever they liked there, especially in the middle where no one could see inside. Lex or Pride as she had to call him, liked having Faith at his side at lunch times even though it meant being near Cyphren and his cult-like followers. His siblings also sat that there, lazing around the table, usually not eating and always the centre of attention.

Faith did not know how she felt about Cyphren or the rest of Nemfora's children. He was no longer unpleasant around her. For the most part, he just ignored her. The only one of Nemfora's children who paid her any attention was the new student, her half-brother Storm.

Storm was just like his name, Faith thought. Unpredictable, a little wild and impossible not to watch. He had skin like a gold statue and muscles to match. In contrast to his large body, his face was kind. He had dark curly hair like Faith, and it was spiralling in all directions around his head completing his look of an ancient statue. That day at lunch, he was sitting on the table spinning something between his fingers that Faith was certain it was something he should not be allowed to have at school but of course, he did have free reign.

"You look bored Storm," Lex commented from beside Faith. She was spooning dollops of chocolate pudding into her mouth while Lex

17

played with a strand of her hair, winding the curl around his forefingers and unravelling it. He had said it was like ASMR to him, calming and soothing to his troubled mind. It did not bother Faith. It made her tingle when he did it, so it was like her ASMR as well.

"Mortal schools are boring," he complained. "The girls are cuter, but I need more stimulation."

"We make our own stimulation here Storm," said Cyphren kissing the girl sitting in front of him on the neck. She squirmed and leaned back into him clearly enjoying the attention.

"I wanna do magic," he sulked still spinning the metal item in his hand.

Every now and then it hovered above his hand but too quickly for anyone to catch it.

"On mortals?" Rain suggested, Faith's other half-brother asked with a wicked grin.

"In general man," he whined. "I wanna break stuff, is that too much to ask?"

"You can break stuff in the old campus," said Faith suddenly and the bright eyes of her Demimage social group snapped to her in surprise.

"You could..." said Cyphren slowly eyeing Faith suspiciously, his eyes lingering on her longer than anyone else's did.

"I sometimes go down there to practice stuff," she explained truthfully. Alexander Prep was an old school with a campus-built underground that was closed off when then-new campus was built as opposed to being destroyed completely though no one knew why.

"Could you show me it?" Storm asked, perking up like an excited puppy. Faith caught Lex's eye and he did not look anxious, so she agreed.

"Yeah, I could show you during our next break," she said licking her spoon clean of pudding.

"Sweet, and you could show me what you've been practicing sis," he said pleasantly. Unlike the only time Cyphren had called her that, when Storm called her 'sis' it sounded like a friendly moniker. Despite herself, Faith liked it. It was hard not to like Storm; he was too much like a puppy who got big too fast but still acted like a kid. He was not bad and did not reek of decay like his other siblings who often feed off humans. She surmised he was like her, daughter of a Fallen but not really interested in Human Energy.

The bell rang and Lex lifted her off the table and set her down. Then he put his tray on top of hers and lifted them both with one hand.

"Shall we?" he said in his deep sexy voice and they set off to Philosophy class hand and hand. As they walked, Faith could feel about a dozen eyes on her and Lex. She had to remind herself that she wanted this to keep from turning around and snapping at them. She wanted to understand her siblings more and get more information about Damiel who she still had not met.

Lex dumped both their trays and exited the dining hall without even a sideways glance behind him. She had to admire his ability to keep his cool in any situation. He gave off this confident air without having to try or come off fake. It was just a part of who he was. As Pride, he was a bit showier and outwardly affectionate but when they were alone and they could be themselves, he was sweet and very patient with her.

They walked hand and hand through the hall and halted at room 301 with Mrs. Matthews, the Western Philosophy teacher.

"Ready to delve into what makes mortals tick?" asked Lex as Pride with a sly grin when Faith heard her name shouted from two classrooms down the hall. She whipped around to see Saoirse bounding towards her, rosy cheeked with ribbons in her braids. She halted in front of them, but Lex gave her a sneer as Pride before releasing Faith's hand and ducking into the classroom without her.

"Faith, have I got a surprise for you," she prefaced as she beamed with glee. Faith rolled her eyes and backed away from her friend.

"Soar, after the last couple of months I've had, I'm done with surprises."

"This is a good surprise, trust me," she said still beaming then she signalled behind her and a tall boy emerged from the crowd of students and scooped Faith up in his muscular arms.

"Hey Fiery, it's been a while," he whispered in her ear sending familiar tingles down her spine.

3

Old Friends

"You can take people who haven't seen each other in years and put them in a room together and the same group dynamics that existed all those years ago, remain exactly the same." - Anonymous

FAITH LET HERSELF BE enveloped by the boy who still towered over her even though she had grown at least half a foot since they last saw each other. He set her back down and swiftly kissed her on the left cheek. Faith felt her face burn where he had kissed her as a dozen or so uniformed students gawked and pointed at the large boy who in his dark casual clothes was clearly not a student there.

The boy straightened up and Faith got a better look at him. It was Mitch, her Mitch of some two years ago. Mitcham Sehyun Kang had not changed much though the years had been kind to him. He was always good looking but had issues with acne that his pale skin did nothing to help and a nose slightly too big for his face, but he had grown into it along with his hair which back then was at his shoulders. Now his pencil straight sable locks reached past his back. His almond eyes still made her heart race whenever she looked into them.

"I can't believe you're here," said Faith staring up at him shaking her head.

"I can't believe I am still so much taller than you," he said chuckling and grinning like a schoolboy. "You weight like nothing too."

'What every girl wants to hear,' thought Faith.

"Mitch is here on a holiday from Korea," said Saoirse, answering the un-asked question.

"Oh, for how long?"

"A couple of weeks which gives us plenty of time to catch up and celebrate your birthday. Didn't think I forgot did you?," he said with a wink then he bent down so that his lips were at her ear. "I've got a lot to tell you."

Faith did not know what to say so she just nodded while sneering at the audience their conversation was making. *'Didn't they have anything better to do?'* It was the consequence of being suddenly popular. Everyone was interested in the new girl who was dating a guy from the most exclusive clique at school. It was an unwanted consequence that made her the subject of blatant stares and open curiosity.

At that moment, the warning bell sounded, and Mitch made a grasp for her hand before she could duck inside the classroom.

"I'll see you after school," he said sweetly then he released her hand and allowed himself to be stirred away by Saoirse who had to get to her own class. Faith gave her an exasperated look that she returned with an apologetic grin. *'What was she thinking bringing him here with everything that is going on?'* she wondered while gliding to her desk next to Pride, their seats unusually close. He was sitting with his arm open waiting for her to slide into it and she did not hesitate. His lips curled into a satisfied smile as she nestled next to him. The showy Pride liked everyone to know Faith was his girlfriend especially the other girls in the room who did not hide the fact that they thought he had made the wrong choice.

Unlike Cyphren who went through girls on a weekly basis, Pride never dated anyone though many tried. Lex explained that Pride 'belonged' to Cyphren and that included an intimate relationship. Faith had to hide her shock when he told her some weeks ago in his apartment.

She was sitting in between his legs resting her head on his shoulder while he read poetry to her when he finally told her about the true nature of his relationship with Cyphren.

"I didn't know," she said hoping he was not hurt by the shock in her voice. She knew it did not matter to their relationship. His feelings for her were evident.

"It's not public knowledge," he said, rubbing her arms soothingly.

"Did you care for each other?" she asked while trying to keep her face straight.

"It was a means to an end Faith. That is all," he said quickly.

"Did he...treat you well?" she asked trying but failing to picture her stepbrother who she has always regarded as despicable, be kind.

"In that regard, yes," said Lex. "He has no reason to mistreat me for I have proved my loyalty to him many times."

"In what regard is he not?" Faith asked half not wanting to know the answer. He was after all her stepbrother. Probably because he sensed it in her or he knows her better than she thought, Lex did not answer. He just wrapped his arms around her and held her tight.

"It's not important because the moment you and I met; I haven't been with him in that way again."

"Not at all?"

"I've thought of nothing but you the moment our eyes met that day after school."

"Really?"

"Truly," said Lex and lifted her head to meet his lips. "I belong to no one but you now."

FAITH RECALLED THE event with some guilt while she thought of the explanation she would have to give him for Mitch and the explanation she would have to give Mitch as well. She saw the question in Lex's eyes when she entered the room, the only part of him that was not Pride. *'How would he take to Mitch?'* she wondered fearfully. The fact that she had a past should not bother him since she knew his. But there was something else about Mitch that she would have to tell him, a secret only she and Saoirse knew, a secret that would put a target on his back.

4

Torrent

"I've told myself a thousand times that I am immune to such feelings. I've never felt them in my life but in that moment, I felt a rage like no other." -
Lex

LEX HAD TO KEEP HIS cool as Pride. Whatever went on in the hallway when Saoirse turned up, he was not supposed to have seen but he did see it and he did listen. Since he found out that Faith had arrived at Alexander Prep, he used Cyphren's connections to find out everything about her that was on record. He knew the name of each school she had attended, the number of school recitals she won and all the old acquaintances she had. Mitchum Sehyun Kang was known to Lex only by name for he was in the school band with her but that was all he knew.

He watched Mitch pick her up, swing her around and kiss her with his insides writhing like snakes. He surmised from their brief conversation and the way he held Faith that they had some kind of relationship before he met her. But his mind raced with questions like *'When did it end? How did it end and who ended it?'* Questions he told himself were none of his business but questions that ate away at him until Faith was back in his arms and paying attention to what the Philosophy teacher Mrs. Mathews was saying.

He did not like this side of him at all; the side that wondered, the side that seethed and the side that hated Mitch. He had to shake those feelings away and try and get to know Mitch or else he would give himself away. Faith did not need to know this side of him not after she had been so understanding when he revealed the true nature of his relationship with Cyphren.

Cyphren was not at all pleased when he learned that Pride would have to date Faith, a sentiment he made perfectly clear one day in Catlinis's office.

"You with Faith?" he fumed not bothering to keep his voice down since the office was blissfully empty save for them and the walls were sound proofed.

"I must do my part for your mother and for our cause," said Lex, his head bowed while he kneeled at Cyphren's feet.

"I know but it doesn't mean I have to like it," he sneered. "You know I don't like to share." At this, Cyphren caressed Lex's jawline affectionately. "I must entertain myself in other ways."

That was the only time he and Cyphren spoke about Faith. In her presence, he deliberately ignored her. This did not bother him for he knew Faith was still uncomfortable being around her step brother. Nemfora's other children did exactly as she ordered, treat her like family to lure her into GARGOYLE. It must have been too much for Cyphren so rather than be openly hostile towards her, he chooses not to interact with her at all.

None of his siblings reported this behavior back to Nemfora and neither did Pride. The children were extremely loyal to each other. A blood bond made stronger by their shared abilities. Lex knew this bond well, it was the bond shared by his twin, Pileah. Their time apart did not sever it. They communicated whenever it was safe. He was close with his other sister Salene but being twins and sharing abilities made his bond with Pileah stronger.

Thinking of Salene then made him remember something he had to ask Faith. A request of sorts that might put them in danger but a request he needed to ask of her. His thoughts were disturbed by Mitch's display of affection towards Faith and it made him more determined to ask her. It would solidify their relationship in his eyes while simultaneously exposing her to a world she might be better off not knowing.

5

Dissonance

IF I COULD GO BACK in time, I would change nothing because the events that led me here, led me to you." – Faith

AFTER SCHOOL THAT DAY, Faith paced up and down the roof top of Tiberius Hall. The little seating area which was once used to eat lunch now did not allow food, so students rarely went up there. It was fenced all around for safety and magicked by Lex to keep out Demimages. Whenever they drew near, they would feel the power of Light and become uncomfortable. It was the perfect place for them to talk privately and be themselves. They went up there whenever they had a free moment from classes.

Today however, Faith did not think they would stick to their normal roof top routine. She had something important to tell Lex that was sure to be a mood spoiler. Faith went over what she was going to say to him in her head, fearful she would mess up if she did not. She stopped mid pacing when she heard his footsteps coming up the stairwell. He flung open the door and she raced into his arms, happy to see him even though they had only been separated for one period. He held her close for a moment then guided her to the white bench in the middle of the roof.

Faith's hand wounded around Lex's fingers when he sat down next to her, wanting to feel his warmth before she spilled her guts about Mitch. Per their normal routine, Lex planted soft kisses from her shoulder to her neck, causing her to squirm involuntarily with delight. Faith had to remind herself that she wanted to talk to him because his kisses were driving all rational thought out of her head.

"Lex, there's something I need to tell you," she started, giving his hand a squeeze and he ceased his kissing.

"About?"

"About someone who has come back into my life today," she said, and she felt him tense up at her side. "I know you were bothered earlier because I felt it when I returned to class. You hid it well from everyone else but not from me." Lex shifted uncomfortably but did not move from his spot next to her.

"You mean that 7 feet tall mass of muscle that picked you up and kissed you on the cheek? What boyfriend would not be bothered by that?" he said, and Faith winced as if he'd struck her.

"You saw?" she asked flushing. It was enough that total strangers saw their exchange, it was quite another thing for the boy she had been dating exclusively for three months to see.

"Of course, I saw."

"How?" she scrutinized, thinking back to the moment, and trying to visualize where she was standing in reference to the open classroom door and where Lex sat.

"How do you think?" he muttered and then it dawned on her and she pulled her hand away from Lex's and glared at him, her eyes blazing.

"You used magic to spy on me?"

"I wasn't going to at first...I just...ahhh. I saw that guy and I do not know. Something inside me told me to watch, for your protection," said Lex running an uneasy hand through his hair as he struggled to get the words out.

"You're really going to use that to justify you spying on me?" This was not how she wanted to introduce the subject of Mitch nor how she wanted her relationship with Lex to be, full of accusations and suspicion.

"I didn't know who that guy was, and he had his hands on you," he argued. "What would you do if a girl you had never seen before suddenly came up and hugged me in broad daylight?"

Faith bit her lip and felt heat building up in her fingertips at the thought of seeing him with another girl. *What would I have done? Could I really blame Lex?* She relaxed slightly and took Lex's hand in hers once more.

"You're absolutely right," she said. "But I don't like the idea of you spying on me Lex. I'm never going to like it, but we are in uncharted territory here and behind enemies' lines. Sometimes you are going to have to watch me for my protection. Just try to trust me more okay?"

"I will," said Lex, bringing her hand up to his lips and kissing it gently with a sad puppy dog look in his eyes that melted her heart and quelled her anger. "Now, will you tell me who that guy was because the way he kissed you didn't seem like he was family."

"That's because he isn't," said Faith slowly. "Mitch is my ex-boyfriend. His name is Mitcham Kang and he was my boyfriend back in Cali." Lex took a deep breath like he was trying to calm himself down before he next spoke, and it made Faith nervous.

"Ex-boyfriend of how long?"

"Two years," said Faith and Lex went from calm to incensed in a matter of seconds, wrenching his hand from hers and standing up.

"Two years?" he repeated, his eyes wide with disbelief "You went out with someone for two years and you didn't think this was something I needed to know?"

"I...I thought about telling you but with him far away in South Korea, I did not think it was relevant to us. To our relationship," said Faith feeling worse than she had when he revealed he'd spied on her. *'This is not going well.'*

"Someone significant in your life seems pretty relevant to me especially by the way he behaved with you today," said Lex icily, his hands fist at his sides. "He is clearly still into you. And more to that, how could you keep that you were in relationship before me after I told you about *my* ex? In months of our conversations, did it not occur to you that I had a right to know about Mitcham just as you had a right to know about Faye?"

Faith did not think about that. True, they talked a lot about their lives either at dinner or alone in his apartment. She told him about adjusting to her powers and growing up having to keep them secret, but the subject of exes never came up. She never imagined he would react this way.

"Mitch was gone Lex," she said standing up and approaching him tentatively. "He was my first boyfriend and he left, just when things with Maurice were getting worse and I started seeing...terrible things in my sleep and in my waking hours. I felt...I felt abandoned...again. First by Maurice and then Mitch. So yeah, I did not tell you about him because it was hard Lex. Just like it was hard for you to tell me about Faye."

Faith turned from him, flexing her fingers to quell her anger and pain before they manifested in a burnt roof top. It was the first time she admitted to herself how hurt she was by Mitch's leaving for South Korea. He was the first man she had let into her heart apart from the man she thought was her father. Their breakup was a teary send off in the International Terminal at LAX.

She hugged herself as a chill ran up her body in the December air. The winter was another reason people did not go on the roof. There was no escape from the cold. While Faith was wishing she had brought her gloves and scarf, she felt strong arms enclose around her and Lex's head in the crook of her neck.

"I'm sorry Faith. I didn't mean to stir up old feelings," he said, his voice soft and full of contrite. "It's just after everything we've been through...we know what secrets and lies can do to a relationship. The thought of you keeping something from me ..."

"It won't happen again Lex," said Faith turning around in his arms so she said could see his face. His eyes were large, and the corners of his mouth were turned down, but his embrace were affectionate and protective. "No more secrets. I'll tell you everything."

He bent low and kissed her lips briefly and it filled her with warmth and reassurance.

"And in the spirit of no more secrets, there is something else you need to know about Mitch, but you have to promise me you won't get angry again. To be fair this isn't my secret to tell but I believe you have a right to know," she prefaced, her hands going to his face and cupping it in her cool hands. He did not say anything, he just nodded and closed his eyes.

"Mitch isn't just my ex-boyfriend who is suddenly back in my life," she started, choosing her words carefully to not rise him again. "Mitch has powers, like us." Lex's flashed open at her words. "But before you jump to conclusions, he isn't a mage. Both his parents are human, and they have no powers. He is just telekinetic. He can move things. Mostly rocks actually. Anything made from stone." Lex was silent for a minute, his eyes moving rapidly in his head as he stared wildly at her.

"I never heard the words 'just' and 'telekinetic' in the same sentence before," he said dryly. "He must be a Chosen."

"A human gifted with powers by the Celestial beings but not a mage?" said Faith remembering her brief lessons as an Affinity member. Lex nodded and pulled Faith closer as a gust of wind ran past them.

"You have to keep him off GARGOYLE's radar," said Lex looking serious.

"What for?" said Faith

"We can't sense Chosen. Their powers are designed to help them blend in and hide in plain sight. Nemfora has people trying to track down Chosen."

"What would they want with Chosen?"

Lex took a deep breath once again and it made Faith nervously bite her lip. *'What could be so serious?'* she wondered.

"Of all the mortals on earth, Chosen have the most potent Human Energy on the planet. If any Demimage found out what he is, he'd be a walking target."

"No," Faith breathed, her head spinning. "You're kidding?"

"I wish I were," sighed Lex. "I've seen groups of demons feeding on a Chosen. Their energy is like steroids. It will power you up significantly and the effects are lasting."

"Just when I thought my life couldn't get any more complicated," said Faith just as the warning bell sounded for after school activities to start. Mitch was probably waiting for her outside the school. Thinking fast, she had to find a way to keep him off any demon's radar. "I'll tell Saoirse. She'll make sure the Affinity keeps watch over him."

"Of course, they can protect him. My aunt...Daia has seen to the protection of Chosen before. She'll know what to do."

"Good, let's get out of here." He grabbed her hand and they glided out the door and down the stairs. Her talk with him had not gone exactly to plan but everything was out in the open now. However, Faith had another difficult discussion ahead of her, telling Mitch about Lex and the Sister's Affinity. *'To think just hours ago I was worried about celebrating my birthday'.*

6

To be Expected

"I can make you love me, and I can make you detest me. But I can I make you worship me?" - Anonymous

Faith left Lex in the internet café to meet Mitch in front of the school. Still reeling from Lex's reaction, she barely focused on anything as she stalked through the halls. She usually kept her head down in the hallways when she was not with Pride. One good reason was because the almost daily ghostly apparitions she saw were easier to ignore if she only saw their floating feet. The other reason was to avoid eye contact with her cold classmates.

Normal people generally stirred clear of what was called 'Cyphren's Crowd.' Since Faith was now considered a member, they stirred clear of her too. Cyphren's Crowd had an intimidating reputation throughout the school. Only people who wanted 'in', sucked up to them.

The mortal boys and girls who hung out with them were treated like snacks by the demons. Miraculously, they did not mind. They knew they were demons and they liked the perks and popularity that coupled being their human companions and there were many. Faith was happy to know that Pride had no such companion. He usually 'fed' with Cyphren. Whatever they did to feed, Faith did not know.

Whispers passed her as she walked through the halls. She caught things like 'Pride's new girl.'

'She is so lucky.'

'I wonder what she did to get in with Cyphren's crowd.'

'Pride can do better.'

'What are you talking about, she's hot.'

'She's stuck up like the rest of them, doesn't even acknowledge us.'

Faith had to ignore their mutterings no matter how much they bothered her. Back in California, she would have thrown one of them clear across the room for their remarks. Just one would have been enough to shut them up. After Faith learned to defend herself, she never let anyone bully her again. Her temper did not help her make friends, but it kept all unpleasantness away from her.

No one at Alexander Prep knew of her past and Lex suggested that she keep it that way. "The last thing we need is people digging into your life," he had said. "You want people to fear you yes, but gradually. You can't turn on a heel. For now, your reputation is neutral. For our plan to work, you have come around to the demon way of thinking naturally."

Faith did not like the idea of students thinking she was soft. She only agreed to Lex's idea after many kisses. "Soon all of them will fear you."

Instead of knocking the wind out of the girl who made the last comment. Faith paused and sent her an icy glare. The girl's face went rigid. She tried to stand her ground but then Faith's eyes flashed, and she flinched. Satisfied, she traipsed down the hall and out to the front of the school where many students were standing around in groups, chatting excitedly about the start of the weekend. Faith scanned the area for Mitch and found him leaning against a cherry red sports car with his arms crossed over his broad chest.

"Did he get more gorgeous in the time we were apart?" Faith muttered as she approached his car. He beamed at her causing a familiar flutter in her heart that she had no control over. Shaking her head of curls, Faith gave him what she hoped was a friendly smile.

"Hey kitten," he said, calling her by her private nickname and Faith was thankful her caramel brown skin did not visibly blush.

"Hey Mitch," said Faith pleasantly. "Where'd you get the car?"

"It's a rental."

"It's nice, it suits you."

"She's a beauty. Wish I could bring her back to Korea with me," he said, petting it affectionately and looking at her with a lopsided grin and a raised eyebrow which made her think he wasn't just talking about the car.

"So, you are going back then?"

"Ah eventually," he said offhandedly. "Korean winters are crazy cold. I miss our California winters with pool parties and walks on the pier."

"Those were the days," Faith agreed. "But New York is not much warmer than Korea is it?"

"It has its perks," he said with a wink. "And central heating."

"Say, could we talk," Faith said suddenly. She did not want to put it off any longer with Mitch winking and hinting at something that was no longer possible.

"About what?"

"About...things that happened when you were away."

"Are these happy things or not so happy things?"

"Depends on how you look at it."

"Why don't I like the sound of that?"

"Oi, you two!"

Faith whipped around to see Saoirse bounding towards the two of them with red cheeks and her necktie eschew.

"Hey Soar," said Faith locking arms with her.

"Sehun is that you bro?!"

Devonte ran right up to Mitch and gave him a one-armed hug, grinning from ear to ear and jumping up and down excitedly.

"Dude what are you doing in New York?"

"Just visiting man."

"I gotta show you around then! This is your ride?"

"Yeah, hop in," said Mitch, opening the door.

"I show all the cool spots to hang around here."

"See you girls later, Saoirse has my number," he added with a squeeze of Faith's shoulder. As soon as he started the engine, the front of the school was full of a bass heavy tune and what Faith recognized as Korean speed rapping. Devonte bobbed to the beat next to Mitch, who waved with his free hand then sped off down the street, the car vibrating with the sound of the bass.

Faith blinked several times as she went over what just happened in her head. She was just about to tell Mitch about everything when Saoirse and Devonte unknowingly interrupted them. It was a like hurricane had passed through leaving Faith stunned in its wake.

She turned to Saoirse and gave her a lopsided look.

"What?" she said shrugging in answer to Faith's expression.

"I was just about to tell Mitch about you know who and the whole shebang when you and Devonte stormed in and now he's gone."

"Oops."

"Yeah and hey why didn't *you* tell him I have a boyfriend?"

said Faith, rounding on Saoirse who held up her hands defensively just as her dad's car pulled up.

"I don't know," she shrugged, as she reached for the car door. "I didn't think it my business hun. Besides, even if I told him about your boyfriend, he would still want to hear it from you."

Faith's face fell, knowing she was right. She slid inside the car and greeted Mr. Abbey cordially but her mind was on her troubles. He and Saoirse went on about school as he drove while Faith had her face in her phone, scanning through Twitter absentmindedly. As much as she would rather Mitch found out about Lex/Pride from someone else, she knew Mitch would want to hear it directly from her lips.

They arrived at Saoirse's townhouse in next to no time and the girls raced to her bedroom. Saoirse jumped right onto her bed with her face planted in her smartphone. Faith sat down beside her with a vacant look in her eyes. She did not want to bring Saoirse more worries but she had to know that Mitch was in danger so she could help protect him.

"What's up Faith?" she asked without removing her gaze from her phone.

"There's something you need to know."

"By the look on your face I am guessing it's not about the two gorgeous men in your life vying for your attention?"

"It's not," she said, slumping her shoulders. "You know how Mitch?has powers yeah?"

"Yes."

"Well it's not just some weird phenomenon. He's a Chosen. A human gifted with abilities by the celestial beings."

"Whoa that's so cool," said Saoirse then Faith raised an eyebrow and Saoirse shook her head. "Not so cool?"

"Not when it puts a target on his back to a pack of demons," said Faith and she hastily explained about the Demimages hunting Chosen."

"Get out, that's unbelievable," said Saoirse, her eyes spinning in her head. "I'll let the girls know first thing tomorrow, we gotta do whatever it takes to protect him."

"Knew I could count on you Soar," said Faith beaming.

"Anytime Fire, anytime."

"Good," she said snapping her fingers and admiring the tiny flame that floated above her finger like it was a lighter.

"Say, how did Lex take to Mitch?" Saoirse asked suddenly and the tiny flame grew to the size of her palm at her question as if tied to her emotions.

"That well huh?"

Faith snuffed the flame with another snap and fell backwards on the bed so that she was face up and gazing at the ceiling.

"He took it terribly," she moaned before delving into the story of their roof top argument.

"You should have seen his face when I told him we dated for two years," Faith recalled guiltily.

Saoirse laid down next to her and slipped her arm around Faith's.

"You had no way of knowing he would react like that hun."

"But you don't blame him for being angry do you?" Faith asked dreading the answer. Saoirse tightened her hold on her arm and bit her bottom lip.

"Well, can you?" she said her eyes wide. "I mean after all the hot nights you two spent curled up in bed together you never once mentioned you dated someone before him?"

"No and what do you mean hot nights?"

"You know," she needled with a nudge. "You and Lex entangled on your bed in a hot fiery..."

"Whoa, whoa, whoa," Faith jumped, sitting up bolt right and Saoirse followed. "Lex and I have never...well that is to say we uh..."

Saoirse's jaw dropped as Faith's words dawned on her.

"You've got to be kidding me," she exclaimed then she dropped her voice to a whisper. "You mean to tell me, all the nights you spent at his house when you were supposed to be here, the two of you never slept together? After three months of dating?" Faith shook her head, wanting to bury it in her hands. It was true, she had spent many nights with Lex, but it had all been PG-13."

"How could you lie next that platinum blond fox and not want to jump him?"

"Soar, you're forgetting we've only known each other days before we started dating. He kissed me the first time we were ever alone together," she said recalling the event in the hallway briefly when he felt compelled to kiss her beyond human reasoning. "As fast as our relationship started, it made sense for me to slow things down and really get to know each other."

"Alright, I see where you're coming from hun," said Saoirse nodding and patting Faith on the shoulder.

"With everything in my life being supernatural, I want things with Lex to progress naturally. Like it was for you and Dev. You guys dated for a year before you slept together, and you knew each other a lot longer before then."

"That's true," Saoirse confessed, her eyes reminiscent as a warm smile spread across her face. "Dev and I clicked immediately but we did wait a while and honey it was worth the wait."

The girls laughed at loud then Faith took Saoirse's hand in her own.

"That's what I want Soar. Fireworks and the true intimacy that comes with really knowing your partner."

"I get that," said Saoirse nudging her friend once more.

"What about you, any hot guys in your view?" Faith asked, hoping mentioning her past relationship with Devonte was not a sore spot still. At her inquiry, Saoirse's ears went pink and Faith needled her for details. "There is isn't there?"

"There is this one guy," she teased, batting her eyelashes rapidly.

"OMG give me the deets. Spill! Does he go to our school?"

"I met him while training in Resora."

"He's a mage?" Faith pressed, her eyes wide and her mouth hanging open.

"Yep, he's a Water Witch like me," she said animatedly. "Oh, the things he can do, wait til I show you all the new tricks he taught me. Did you know there's a way to eavesdrop with water?"

"That sounds so cool."

"He said eventually he'd teach me how to Water teleport," said Saoirse, her eyes sparkling.

"Wait, what's his name? What does he look like?"

"His name is...don't laugh. It's Caspian."

Faith stifled a giggle, her hand pressed to her lips. "Like the Prince?"

"Like the sea!"

Faith giggled furiously at her side and yelped when Saoirse's finger dug into her ribs.

"Listen to us," said Faith, settling down. "Two witches talking about boys like normal teenagers."

"Whouda thunk it?"

There was a soft knock at the door while the girls giggled on the bed.

"Supper is ready," came Mr. Abbey's kind voice from the hallway.

"Coming Da!" said Saoirse grabbing her friend's hand. "Oh, and by the way, I told Da why you've been sleeping here so often."

"What?" said Faith, stopping in her tracks. Saoirse pulled her hand close and squeezed it.

"Don't worry, I left out the supernatural details. He was wondering why you were you spending so much time here, so I told him you'd recently found out you were adopted and that you and the Andrews were struggling to cope with it. That you felt uncomfortable there."

It was not exactly a lie. For all intents and purposes, she was adopted by the Andrews and their current arrangement was not ideal.

"Are you cross with me?" Saoirse asked snapping Faith out of her reverie.

"Of course, not sweetie," she answered as she made for the door. "You had to tell him something. I'm just glad I didn't have to do it. Thanks." Lately her talks were not going too well, and she would hate for Mr. Abbey to find out where she was really spending her nights when she was not there.

"I've got your back Fiery, like always."

Faith grinned at Saoirse, holding back her emotion as she was overcome with affection. Feeling lighter than she had in days, Faith waltzed hand and hand out the door and down the stairs to the kitchen.

7

Deceptive Cadence

"There's only so much that can be endured," - Lex

For years, Alexei Cloud Skye had to be subjected to the most depraved mages he had ever encountered through the course of his work for Nemfora. He was given special permission by the Higher Order to commit crimes that would have gotten him shut in a hanging dungeon for decades. "Anything to bring Nemfora down," his father Cloud had said. Being crown Prince did help with his undercover work as a Demimage. The High Born like him were given special powers at birth that manifested when they came of age. They were powers to help them govern their people when they assumed the thrones of their parents. Powers his younger sister Lordona craved.

There were many illusionists among the Light Mages of varying abilities, but Lex could do something few could not. He could cast a demonic glamour that would allow him to fool even Nemfora into believing he was a full-fledged Demimage when in fact, Lex had never fully absorbed Human Energy. At least, not enough to change him. He did feed on mortals, but he did it in a clever way that made it impossible for it to corrupt him, but it was not easy, and it was terribly taxing. If not for his desire to return home one day, he would have succumb to the demon side years ago. It was the memory of his wife Faye and his child that gave him the strength to carry on. Now it was Faith. A chance at happiness. A chance at a family again. Faith offered him something he thought he would never regain again.

So, when he had heard that she once loved another before him, he could not control the hurt and the jealously that came along with that knowledge and he lashed out at her. *She must think me a brute,* he thought bitterly as he leaned against the Internet Café door while waiting for Cyphren. He had had to make it up to her somehow.

"What's got you so pensive today Pride?" came the sickly-sweet voice of Caprice Leah Landis. She leaned provocatively against the opposite wall watching him. How long she was there, he had no idea. She was a Princess herself and could have used a number of abilities to hide from him. Today she had her hair in twin tails completing her look of a cartoon character.

"I have a lot on my mind your Highness," he answered gruffly not wanting to get into with her. "But it's nothing I will trouble you with."

"It's no trouble, we are all working together here aren't we?" she said sideling over to him and causing near collisions as students ducked out of her way to avoid her.

"I just want to feed before returning to my duties at the castle," he lied.

"As you wish," said Cyphren in a honeyed voice as he appeared suddenly at his side. Lex bowed to him in greeting.

"Where would you like to feed today," he asked cordially.

"Nothing special today," said Cyphren disappointment clear in his voice. "I have a couple of tasty treats waiting for us in the student council office."

"Let's go," said Pride clapping his hands enthusiastically.

The student council was full of mortals who craved Cyphren's attention no matter how much it endangered them. Mortals with knowledge of the magical world were not many but they did exist. Most times, they grew up amongst mages in known magical communities. Some acted as liaisons between worlds and worked tirelessly to keep our secrets from the greater mortal public.

There were also low lives and greedy businessmen who wanted magical ways to do more even more evil or earn them more profit. This is how Demimages made their fortunes and gained influence. Mortals at the top of the metaphorical food chain would offer up their own people to be fed on by demons in exchange for favors. Nemfora greatly approved of this because it saved a lot of time and bother.

At school, it made it possible to obtain Human Energy without the risk of exposure by feeding on unwilling mortals. Lex detested feeding on humans no matter what the circumstance but feeding from a willing participant was a moral grey area he had to trample on.

"What are our duties when we return to the castle?" Lex asked in too low a voice to carry.

"Recruitment," Cyphren groaned. "You know our Queen has this big operation soon, so we need all the troops we can get."

"Understood," said Lex. Recruitment meant they would have to go Dorcela, the only perk. He like Cyphren detested recruiting for various reasons. The slaughtering of innocents being the major reason and spewing Nemfora's twisted views in a believable voice being the other. What Lex knew of this 'big operation' was vague but he knew it involved a major official. Working so closely with Cyphren meant he could subtly ask for information about the op. The more he knew about it, the better equipped the Brotherhood would be at stopping it. Some sacrifices had to be made of course. Some operations had to be successful or Nemfora would suspect a mole. The Brotherhood had to weigh the collateral damage in order to bring Nemfora's organization down. Ridding the world of Nemfora was not as simple as destroying her. The whole of GARGOYLE had to be dismantled so that no one would rise up to take her place.

Lex entered the student council room to find three mortals waiting for them: student body president Josephine, the basketball star Charles and the student treasurer Tiffany. Josephine approached Lex with a wide smile and her hair pulled back from her neck. It was not necessary to feed from that area, it was just easier. In truth, Human Energy could be obtained from any part of the body, but the neck offered easy access. Josephine turned around in front of him and waited. The other reason people preferred this way was because they did not have to see them transform while the demons fed from their necks.

Lex murmured chants in his head to start the illusion as he pulled the girl close by her shoulders. Unseen by her, his skinned darkened, tiny horns erupted from his head and his entire body was enveloped by black flames. It was a grotesque form he detested. A punishment from the celestial beings for engaging in this forbidden exchange. Lex put his lips to the girl's throat and a purple substance oozed from her pores like mist. The process of keeping up the illusion drained his own energy as he fake drained Josephine. It was necessary to absorb enough of her energy to replenish him and weaken her but luckily it was not enough to change him. *Another perk of being High Born,*' he said gratefully in his mind. A normal Light Mage would be turned by just a couple of sessions of feeding.

Lex felt the girl's legs give and he held her up, the illusion not over. Tiffany and Charles were already slumped over in their demon's grasps as they were more eager feeders. Wincing as the smell of decay reached his nostrils, Lex hoped desperately that Faith would never have to witness him feeding.

8

A Fiery Fortissimo

"My temper flares up and down like a ball. It has taken me years to control it properly. I fear one day I will be so angry that I burn everything around me to cinders." – Faith

AFTER SCHOOL ON MONDAY, Faith exited the main school building with a determined stride. She ignored the whispers and the looks and basked in the glow of being popular. On the advice of Lex, Faith decided to take a different approach to her classmates.

"Eventually you want them to fear you," he said on Saturday evening. She left Saoirse's house and found Lex parked down at the far end of the road. He greeted her with a kiss that left her eager for more. The caress of his soft lips on hers, the gentle pressure, and the brief slip of his tongue in her mouth combined to make her moan appreciatively. She felt him smile against her lips before he released her and set off for his home.

"Say, I heard that you growled at Summer Stevens on Friday," said Lex as he slipped Faith's right hand into his at the red light.

"I did what to who?"

"Summer Stevens said you growled at her the hallway after school."

Faith racked her brain then she remembered those students whispering in the halls about her. They were not to know that she had heightened senses due to her feline spirit form. But she did not like what they were saying, and she retaliated in the tamest way she could.

"Oh her," said Faith rolling her eyes. "Girl is lucky I didn't throw her through a wall."

"That she is."

"Did I really growl at her? I thought I glared in her general direction."

"Your spirit form must have taken over in your anger," Lex surmised releasing Faith's hand for a moment to make a left turn.

"Oh, I'll keep that in mind if there's a next time," mumbled Faith. "You don't think I overreacted do you?"

"Not at all. You want them cowering to you eventually. You should walk the hallways like you own the place."

"Like Cyphren and my 'siblings' do?" she said rolling her eyes again.

"Yes, I know you've got it in you. It's time they did too."

"Alright. I'll give it go as they say."

"And they will marvel at you."

"That's all I want," said Faith loftily, lifting her chin slightly.

"What did Summer say to you to set you off anyway?"

Faith bit her inner lip and gazed out of the window. "Something about wondering what you saw in me."

Lex brought Faith's hand to his lips and kissed it.

"What I see in you is a fearless, driven and gorgeous Firestarter with a warm heart and a bit of a temper."

"Ha Ha, funny," said Faith but she felt her heart leap at his words.

"But honestly, you shouldn't let girls like that get to you," Lex cautioned. "You're a couple of temper tantrums away from setting the school a blaze. You want them to fear you not call the cops on you."

"I hear you Lex I'll try and keep it in check."

Back in the present, Faith took Lex's words to heart. She no longer kept her head down in the halls. She did not strut like she was Carrie Bradshaw, but she held her head high and acted like the others did not exist. Faith exited the school to find Storm sitting alone on the edge of the decorative fountain with a vacant look in his amber eyes. Taken aback, she approached him, and he did not move so she sat down next to him.

"What's up Storm?"

"Oh, hey sis."

"You alright?" she asked, examining him. He was not his usual loud and bumbling self. His eye lids drooped and there was a definite slump to his broad shoulders.

"Hmm?"

"You're underfed," she commented, finally recognizing the symptoms. Demimages who go long without Human Energy look vacant and downcast.

"I'll feed eventually," he said dispiritedly. There was something else bothering him Faith thought but she could not put her finger on what it was. She decided to try and get it out of him.

"You don't like feeding often do you?"

"You're one to talk," he said, rounding on her but keeping his voice low. "You don't feed at all, not that you need to. You're the daughter of a Star and I know you inherited some of father's abilities. I'd have to drain a handful of humans to get close to your level."

"Would you?" Faith did not know how powerful she was having never fully tested her abilities for fear of burning down buildings. "What's so great about Human Energy anyway?" she pressed.

Storm looked up, his eyes on the sky above them and not her. He seemed to be thinking of a way to answer her.

"Picture its summertime," he started still not looking at her. "You're on the beach and its sweltering hot. Beads of sweat break out over your skin, your arms, your forehead, and the back of your neck. You get in the water to cool down, maybe you swim or surf." Faith could not see how any of this had to do with Human Energy, but she listened intently anyway.

"Now, instead of quenching your thirst with water or ice cream, you quench it with Human Energy and suddenly you no longer feel the heat," he said with a kind of manic gleam in his eyes. "The sweat disappears from your skin. You feel like you could run a mile. You get in the water and ride the tallest waves known to man that could crush a human with no effort whatsoever. You can lift a car without breaking a sweat and do it all with a smile on your face. Food taste better, everything is sweeter, everything is heightened. You could go days without sleep on a full draining."

"So basically, it temporarily turns you into Superman?" said Faith.

"Basically. It's the best hit there is and it's right there for the taking. No feeling in the world compares to it."

"I can think of one," said Faith out of the corner of her mouth thinking of Lex and she felt in his arms. Then a wistful look on Storm's eyes made her pause and stare at him. She knew that look. It is how she looked when she was around Lex and that is when she realized it.

"You're in love," she said, and Storm put a hand to her mouth to silence her, but it was not firm.

"Keep your voice down!"

"You're in love," she whispered when he removed his hand. "That's why you haven't been feeding."

"She doesn't like the smell," he said, wrinkling his nose.

"She's human?"

"Yeah, and don't tell the others."

"I won't," she said firmly feeling like this was the first real conversation she had ever had with her half-brother. At that moment, Faith looked at him more warmly than she ever had before.

"Is there a way to mask the smell?"

"There is," he said offhandedly. "I just don't...want to feed too often alright." His defences were up, and it was cute she thought.

Just then she saw Mitch's car pull up in front of the school and she stood up.

"You should head back inside," she suggested as nonchalantly as she could manage as she did not want him to see Mitch. "The others will wonder where you are?"

"Yeah, you're right," he said, getting to his feet. "Thanks."

"For what?" He did not answer, he just grinned and walked away with his hands in his pockets. Faith stared after him for a moment then she sped towards Mitch's car. He had gotten out and was leaning against it in his usual cool demeanor making several girls in the vicinity stop and stare.

"Hey Mitch," she greeted him. "Thanks for coming."

"You said it was important," he said looking down at her but there was no twinkle, no flirtatious air.

"It is. Um where do I start?" she said as she peered around to make sure no one was near enough to hear them.

"If this is about your new boyfriend Devonte already told me."

Faith froze. She had not expected that. Of course, Devonte would have said something. They were like brothers.

"Wish I could have told you but am relieved you finally know."

"He treats you alright?"

"He treats me very well."

"Then that's all I need to know," he said holding his hands up in front of him to halt anymore explanation. "Devonte also told me you're some kind of super powerful witch and that Saoirse's in a coven."

"He what? Oh, when I get my hands-on Dev," she growled.

"Speak of the witch," said Mitch, looking towards the school. Faith spun around and sure enough Saoirse was drifting their way with Ambrosia and Catrianna in tow. Two members of the group she was once a member of herself. The group that her mother belonged to which ultimately resulted in her death. Not wanting to see them, Faith turned back to Mitch.

"I gotta take off," she muttered quickly.

"But Saoirse's coming."

"She'll explain everything. I have orchestra practice. See you later."

Faith walked back towards the entrance, her strut returning, and she caught Catrianna's icy gaze and saw something flash in her hands. Catrianna had been unpleasant since the day she met her and was glad to be shot of her. Leaving quickly before she could lose her temper, she heard Mitch greet the girls cordially.

"Hi ladies."

"Hey, these are my friends," said Saoirse brightly. "This is Ambrosia Lioney."

"And I am Catrianna Belle," she said in a deep sultry voice. Cringing, Faith was glad to get out of ear shot.

9

Tristesse

"I thought I had already come to terms with my cold relationship with my father. We will never be close but something in me will always want his approval. - Anonymous

Two weeks passed with little change in Faith's routine. She went to school during the day she practiced her magic with Lex during break times. Stayed at Lex's house during the week unless he was gone for an extended period of time and spent the weekend at Saoirse's. She had only been home to the Andrews house twice. Faith found that she missed her things, her starry night bed sheets. Her fluffy blue slippers and her starry night light. One evening while she was folding her laundry, she recalled the last happy memory with the man she thought was her father, Maurice.

It was her 13th birthday, the day he gave her the night light. She was lying in bed admiring it and he explained why being 13 was so special.

"Being 13 is like being on the cusp of something great," he had said. "You're not a kid anymore. You're a teenager now and I'm sure you think silly things like night lights are childish. But this starry night light is a reminder of what's twinkling above you and blanketing the earth. Stars are special. They can grant wishes and make your dreams come true."

"But we can't see them here in the city," Faith moaned.

"That's why I got you night light, so you won't forget they are there, that they are always there watching over you."

Recalling that memory now hit very differently for Faith than before she found out the truth about everything and about her mother.

"Faith?" said a voice behind her and she jumped and fumbled folding a blanket. She relaxed when she realized it was her uncle Philip. "Yes, Uncle Phil?" she said kindly, turning back to folding. "How you are holding up?" he asked sitting down on her neat bed. Faith just shrugged but not in a rude way. She could not be rude to Philip who had always been so good to her. He was more of a father to her than Maurice ever was. Maybe that is why it was easier to stay away, she wondered. She missed their after-school talks and their lively musical debates. It all seemed awkward and forced now.

"Are you enjoying staying with the Abbey's?"

"It's okay," she said. "They've been really generous."

"Do they understand what's going on?"

"They know the gist."

There was a moment of silence where Faith just lifted a top up and down after it had already been folded. She wanted to burst into tears right there at the family she lost and knew she would never get back. No matter how pleasant they were with each other now, things would never been the same between them and she knew it. She told herself, eventually she would start coming home less and less.

"Would you feel better if we let you get your own place?" her Uncle Philip asked suddenly, and Faith dropped the top she was folding.

"My own place?" she repeated in such a low voice it was like she worried the offer would go away if she said it any louder.

"Under your mother's name perhaps," he suggested. "She did live here."

"That's right, New York was her home too," she said in a faraway voice. "You guys would really do that for me?" Faith asked, her eyes on the stars silhouetted against the far wall.

"We owe you so much for keeping everything from you and this way you wouldn't inconvenience the Abbeys anymore," he said, with a look in his brown eyes that told him these weren't his words even if they were true.

"Maurice put you up to this didn't he?" she accused him, her eyes still on the stars.

"It was his idea but as your guardians it was our idea to go along with it," he said, placing a hand on her shoulder. She almost pulled away, but she could not. She could not hurt her uncle like that.

"How would it even work?" she asked, pulling away as gently as possible and pretending to put her laundry away but she was not really paying attention to what she was doing.

"There's a serviced apartment complex near your school. Sort of like living in a hotel but the room is always yours," he said. "There's a bedroom kitchen and living room as well as study so you can do your homework and practice your music without disturbing other people who live in the building. It works because we can be sure you are safe and looked after. The building is well secured, and you'd be fed three times a day and someone will come around now and then to clean."

"Who'd pay for all this?"

"Maurice set up a special account," he explained. "It's paid for until you graduate from school and you can renew it if you wish or move out."

'I guess guilt makes you do odd things,' she thought to herself. Maurice was basically giving her a blank check. She told herself nothing, but guilt would make him do something so outrageous. He had not contacted her at all since the day he revealed she was not his daughter. She supposed he was with her half-sister Hope. Hope who promised to keep in touch with her proved to be just as much of a disappointment as her father. Not wanting to think about that topic any further, she decided to accept Maurice's offer. If nothing else, it would keep her from having to come back and forth and lie to the Abbey's about where she was, and they could stop pretending to be family.

"Well, what do you think?"

"I'll take it," she said, her face in her closet. She didn't want him to see the tears that now stung her eyes.

"I see," he said but he didn't sound happy or sad. He did not sound anything. "We'll make all the arrangements and move your things in before you go so you won't unpack everything on your own in the middle of your studies."

"Thanks," she muttered, making lots of unnecessary noise in her walk-in closet until she was sure he was gone, then she collapsed into the basket of laundry and let the tears flow freely and silently.

IT TOOK THREE DAYS to get Faith fully situated into her new lonely abode on 5th avenue. The Andromeda Suites were nothing like she expected. Outside it looked like all the other brick buildings in the vicinity. But inside the lobby was like a marbled dream house complete with a door man and elevator attendants, a least a half a dozen fountains and an arched ceiling.

Her suite was on the 5th floor and she was escorted to it by the manager, a thin man with a bit too much mustache and not much hair on his head. He unlocked the door for her and handed her a pair of silver keys which she pocketed.

He let Faith in first and upon entering, she stopped dead when a man wearing a crisp suit and a weak smile turned to face her in the brightly lit living room.

"Hello Faith," said Maurice kindly but the kindness did not reach his face. The manager gabbed quickly about how to use everything while Faith stared at the man in front of her. He went over all the appliances including the silver rotary phone, the ice machine on the fridge, the settings on the thermostat and the times for her serviced meals.

Then he nodded to Maurice and left the room with a soft click of the door closing. Faith wasted no time in clutching the pendant that lay flat against her neck, wondering when she would get to use it.

"You look good," said Maurice fidgeting with his maroon tie.

"You look uncomfortable," said Faith before she could stop herself.

"We haven't seen each other since...," he coughed and did not continue.

Faith rolled a curl between her fingers and looked anywhere but at Maurice. She had so much she wanted to say to him, but she had to weigh it with how much she wanted him gone so he could not force her undealt feelings to resurface. Faith felt her anger ebb and flow like waves on a beach. She could feel the flames building up in her fingers, but she had to hold them back like everything else she was feeling.

"Why are you here now?" asking the question on the top of her list. "A final farewell before you drop me off here? Goodbye and good riddance?"

"I brought you here," he started with an eye twitch. "To this apartment because this is where your mother lived when she went to Alexander Prep."

"Mom lived here?" she exclaimed, her eyes snapping to Maurice.

"Her home was in Dorcela so when she infiltrated GARGOYLE she was put up in this building, in the room even. Built by her parents and named after your grandmother."

"Andromeda."

Faith met her paternal grandmother only once. The eve of her 13th birthday. Faith found her so regal and impressive that she hardly felt worthy of being in her presence. She wore an off-white suit dress that looked like it had been made for her and a jeweled head band that highlighted the curled bun sitting atop her head. She had on a pair of off-white pumps and her nails were expertly manicured. She knew her grandparents were more well off than the Andrews, but they did not tell her how impressive her grandmother was.

She arrived in the afternoon before her birthday party with a box of gifts from her relatives.

"It's so nice to finally meet you Faith," she said, and she actually looked it. "Your grandfather couldn't be here. He is not well enough to travel but he had your mother's favorite cake baked for you."

"Thank you grandmother," she said timidly feeling like she ought to curtsy. Her cousin Devonte hovered on the stairs of their Pacific Palisades home and sniggered at her half shyness. She knew very little about her grandparents other than that they owned lots of real estate and resided in Florida for the weather was better for her grandfather's health. They sent letters and presents every year but that was the first time her grandmother had ever made the long journey to California to see her.

Most of the presents she brought were practical things like a new furniture set for her bedroom, a new computer, and a set of fountain pens. The only gift she still had from that visit was the ring on her left middle finger; a gold band with 7 precious stones set in the middle in the shape of an arch. Faith liked it so much because it looked like a single flame lit on her finger especially when it caught the light.

"Is anything you told me about my grandparents true?" Faith demanded to know as the ring glittered on her finger.

"They do live in Florida on and off between there and Dorcela," he said without a trace of an apology in his voice. "They do own real estate. Your grandfather is really ill, but the illness is magical."

"So, they are mages too?"

He just nodded but then he opened his mouth like he was going to say something and then promptly shut it.

"What?" Faith asked with a bark not wanting anything left to be said between them.

"You should know...they never approved of you not being told who you are," he said with a slight droop of his eyes. "But you were left to me not them. You were given my name."

"Why though," Faith breathed through trembling lips.

"Because I loved Chryselda so much, I would have done anything for her." His voice was pained and gravelly, but his stance was business like, and Faith was ready for this to be over.

"But you couldn't love the daughter that wasn't yours," she said looking away from him. "That's where you failed her and me. Goodbye f... Maurice."

"Goodbye Faith, I wish you the best of luck," he added "And so does Hope."

"Who you won't let me see," she surmised but he did not deny or confirm it as he headed out the door and with that, he was gone. She waited until she could hear his footsteps fading before she clutched her pendant tightly and called out for Lex.

"Lex, I need you," she whispered. It took less than two minutes for him to appear by her side and half a beat for her to fall into his arms. He did not say anything, he just held her for a long moment. Faith held on to him firmly, her arms enclosing around him. She needed him near when she felt like breaking and he held her together just like she hoped he would.

"You came," she whispered unable to hide the relief in her voice.

"Of course, I did," he said, lifting her head with his finger so that he could meet her eyes. She was not crying, yet but she knew he could see the strain in her wrinkled eyes. "I can't believe he brought you here."

"Oh right, you must have been here with mom," said Faith, pulling from his embrace and winding her fingers around his hand.

"It was a lot different back then," he said looking around at the many high-tech appliances like they were alien artefacts. "They remolded it 5 years ago. It used to be more old fashioned."

"Really?"

"Yeah, it was very old New York, vintage style but the managing partners decided to modern the place up after the bookings started to drop. This was her room, but everything is different." Lex's free hand caressed the kitchen counter and fiddled with the complicated buttons of the oven. "This was her little escape from Dorcela."

"Now it's where I am to be exiled," Faith muttered with trembling lips as a vision of girl and boy in rags appeared before her and were gone with a blink of the eye. *I guess this place being old explains why I've seen three apparitions since I've been here. Will I ever feel this is my home?* The tears she held back in front of Maurice finally spilling over and Lex rushed back into her arms. "Why does no one want me? Why do they always leave me?" Faith sobbed on Lex's neck and he patted her back sympathetically.

"I want you Faith," said Lex firmly. "And I'm not going anywhere."

Faith nodded but the tears did not stop flowing. Eventually Lex had to scoop her up in his arms and place her in bed where she spent most of the night spooning her while she wept.

10

Ballad

"I can't control what I feel when I am near her and I've all but given up trying." – Lex

LEX SLEPT AT FAITH'S new home that night and she was incredibly grateful for it. Afraid she would have cried herself to sleep if he wasn't by her side all night. They ate a hearty breakfast at the kitchen bar. It was not a simple breakfast by any means; there were large buttery croissants, toast, scones with three different spreads, milk, orange juice, tea, coffee, bacon, sausages, and eggs of varying types.

"That was a meal," said Lex wiping his mouth free of orange juice and grinning at her. She got the feeling he was trying to cheer her up, but she was staring at the empty glass of orange juice with wary eyes.

"Can you gargle or brush your teeth after that?" Faith insisted, leaning away from him.

"Huh? What for?" he asked, rising from the bar stool.

"I'm allergic to oranges."

"You never told me that," he said, marching to the bathroom but not before shooting her a crooked look.

"It never came up," Faith called after him. "We usually have tea at your place." He grunted and Faith chuckled before getting to work on clearing the kitchen. She tucked most of the leftovers in the handy Tupperware she found in the in the cabinets. Humming while she worked, she could not help thinking blissfully about a future with Lex and wondering if this was practice. She forced the image away as if she were scared it would not happen if she focused on it too much.

Grabbing her pre-buttered and jammed croissant, she headed back to the bedroom where everything from the Andrews house apart from the furniture had also found a new home. Her starry bed sheets, mountains of books, her violin and because she could not leave it behind, her night light.

She hopped back in bed, munching on the large croissant. Lex emerged from the bathroom minty fresh and tousle haired. He joined Faith on the bed, but he did not get under the covers with her.

Faith popped bits of croissant into her mouth while Lex lay next to her, his head on her lap. While she ate, Faith marveled at the beautiful boy before her. With all that was wrong and crazy in her new life in New York, she had Lex. One of the few bright spots.

Popping the last piece of the buttery pastry into her mouth with a flare, a flake fell onto Lex's cheek.

He promptly picked it up and put it into his mouth with a smile. Faith giggled and bent low to meet his lips, her tongue swirling around his warm mouth minty mouth with the sweet taste of butter and strawberry jam. He moaned appreciatively at the upside-down kiss and maneuvered his body until he was kneeling in front of her, their lips leaving each other's for mere moments.

Feeling bold, Faith pulled Lex closer by any part of him she could reach until he was straddling her. His lips left her and trailed kisses from her cheek to her ear lobes down to her neck and Faith trembled with delight at his touch. She squirmed as his lips found her collarbone and his hands pushed the fabric of her silky blue pajamas away from her shoulders. Igniting sounds, she never uttered before, Faith clung hungrily to the boy in her arms, her lips at his ears, his lips driving her crazy.

Just when Faith thought she would lose herself completely, she heard a buzzing and Lex froze. Pride's cell phone was vibrating on the bedside table. And then something thin and gold flew out of Lex's hand. Seconds later, he was holding the phone. He rolled off her and scanned the message rapidly. Faith pulled the covers up to her neck as if whoever was on the other end could somehow see her.

"I'm being summoned," he said, his face falling, and he rose from the bed.

"Summoned where?" said Faith glowering.

"To the castle," he informed her. "Something must be up because Cyphren knows I am with you today." Lex's light eyes were over bright.

"Nothing to do with us I hope."

"I don't think so, this has to do with Nemfora. I have to go."

"I know," said Faith unable to hide the disappointment in her voice.

"I'll be back as soon as I can get away, I promise."

"I know."

Lex cupped her face in his hands and gave her a kiss that would make her knees buckle before he dressed quickly and disappeared out the door.

Sighing, her bed still warm from their earlier actions, Faith needed something to take her mind off what could possibly send Lex flying out of her door so quickly. She also wanted to avoid thinking about what very nearly happened between her and Lex. It was the first time they had ever come that close to being intimate with each other and she did not want to stop him. In fact, she was certain that if Pride's phone had not interrupted them, they would have gone all the way.

Faith reached into the drawer of her bedside table and pulled out the one thing that was sure to get mind off what almost happened and that was a meticulously crafted leather-bound journal with a golden ring printed on it. Her mother's diary. Cracking it open to the last place she read several weeks ago, she lay the book on her lap and started reading.

"It's late spring and I am being called back home by my parents to attend the wedding of my dutiful sister. Every important person in the whole kingdom has been invited. My parents could not be happier. Unlike

their wild demon fighting daughter, my sister Lucia was marrying into one of the wealthiest families around and gaining an important title."

"*Lucia's wedding dress was handcrafted by the best. Caterers were called from all over Dorcela and her fiancé Malcom was being welcomed at my father's side. I am happy for her certainly, I just don't see marriage in my future. At least not in my immediate future. I am still a girl in the eyes of our people. A powerfully blessed girl yes but still an adolescent. There is still so much I want to see and experience before I tie myself down to anything or anyone. I equate the word 'wife' to the word 'property', and I have no present desire to be either."*

"*I of course had to bless the wedding as the Star of Dorcela. The Scepter of Dorcela presided with my second The Shield of Dorcela by my side the entire night like a watch dog. I know it's her job to protect me but goodness she can be overbearing. My gown was so heavy with armor its miracle I could even walk. I know public appearances are the easiest way to assassinate a member of the Celestial Triumvirate, but does she honestly think our enemies would try something on Lucia's wedding day when the entire guard would be in attendance? And besides, she's forgetting I have the inside track on the enemy's movements. A surprise attack would be the best strategy but Nemfora is no fool. She wants to weaken Dorcela's forces by extending hers, not by attacking highly anticipated weddings which would surely make my sister a martyr and that is the last thing Nemfora wants."*

"*She wants followers. She wants people to join her willingly and slaughtering innocents will not provide her with them. No, Nemfora wins through manipulation. By convincing people that her way is the right way and our ways are outdated and unnecessary. That is the root of her recruiting speeches and how she has won over the hearts of thousands."*

Faith closed the book with a creak and pondered her mother's words. Lex explained what the Celestial Triumvirate was when she asked him about the Star of Dorcela.

"Think of the Celestial Triumvirate like both a religious symbol and a governing body with the Star in the middle as the face," he said that evening while they cuddled on the roof top of his apartment complex, surrounded by hundreds of stars. The sight of them enhanced by Lex's magic. "The people look to the Star for council, for blessings, for wisdom. She is the voice of the Celestial Beings."

"Wow," said Faith her eyes on the skies.

"The Scepter is the is the governing body. They make sure all the rules opposed by the Celestial Beings are upheld. They are the head of state of the Higher Order. The Shield is head of the guard and the official protector of the Star. As mages lives are long, these positions can be held for many years. But once the Star passes on and Ascends to the heavens, a new Star must be on hand so there are what we call potentials. Your mother was once one."

"Potentials makes me think of that sci-fi movie," Faith mutter with a raised eyebrow and Lex chuckled.

"Yes, well unlike that film, these potentials display hints of being a Star by exhibiting abilities unique to the Star, abilities that help them perform their duties. You are essentially born a Star, but your powers will not fully mature until you come of age. When it is confirmed, you become a Star in Waiting. Your mother took over as the Star when she was very young because the former Star, your great aunt passed on unexpectedly from a disease unique to our people."

Faith briefly wondered if seeing apparitions was a sign of being a potential, but she did not dare to ask.

"Did my mother enjoy being the Star?" Faith could not help asking. It seemed like a taxing position, being the mouthpiece of your creator.

"She..." Lex paused, and Faith elbowed him to continue. "She never dreamed she would be chosen so soon. It was a great shock."

Faith tried to imagine her mother, a young witch adjusting to her powers and the knowledge that someday she would have to fulfil a destiny she never asked for. *'That's why she called it a cage and why joining the Sister's Affinity must have appealed to her so much,'* she guessed.

Now with her mother's diary in her hands, she was slowly learning more and more about her and the culture of Dorcelians. Faith wondered how her mother would have felt knowing that she was reading her diary. Looking up at the ceiling and imagining the stars, Faith tried to picture her, but the picture was fuzzy. Maurice had only one photo of her in the house and it was a school photo. The young Chryselda looked a lot like her; crazy long hair, cat eyes and an annoyed expression on her opaline face. While gazing at the ceiling, the image of her sister Hope floated into her mind and her smile faded. 'I want to see you," she whispers to no one but for some reason Faith felt like her sister was calling to her just as she was thinking about their mother and Faith was determined to answer that call no matter what it took.

Part Two

Destruction

11

Unacceptable

"I learned long ago to only trust my family. My blood and my brood." -
Anonymous

L ex teleported to the castle as soon as he shut Faith's door. He
reappeared in his chambers and changed quickly into Dorcelian
attire before he magicked himself to the throne room where there was
utter chaos. Demimages yelling across the hall, tensions high, shouting
back and forth.

Nemfora was sitting on her grand golden throne with her children
sitting in smaller but almost at elegant thrones on either side of her.
Storm and his siblings on the left, Cyphren and his siblings on the
right. Lex noticed there were two empty seats beside Nemfora. Damiel
and Flammare were missing. Nemfora's other children were either too
young to be a part of GARGOYLE or had no interest.?

"Stop this at once!" Boomed Nemfora who shot a blast of smoke
into the ceiling silencing the crowd. Her eyes narrowed at the two men
kneeling at her feet that Lex had not noticed earlier. He recognized
them as Crymea and Felix, members of the family guard. Lex could
practically feel the fear coming off them as they hung their heads before
their Queen.

"What happened?" Lex whispered to Aubrey who was standing in
front of him.

"Lady Flammare's been attacked."

"Explain to me how my daughter came to be injured?" Nemfora
asked, her words and voice were light, but the danger was in her eyes
which were an electric blue. Every member of GARGOYLE knew
to leave the immediate vicinity when her eyes turn white. Blue was

a warning sign. She could render everyone within a 15-foot radius around herself, unconscious when her eyes were white. It was for this reason that the guards were the only Demimages in front of Nemfora.

"We were on a recruitment assignment in the Ozmone when were set upon by Light Mages," said Crymea, head still bowed.

"How many?" At that moment, Felix rose into the air as if pulled by marionette strings. He did not scream but his hands clutched his throat and his eyes were straining. Lex recognized the symptoms of Nemfora's blind choke. Torturing Felix while she questioned Crymea.

"We were outnumbered your Grace," simpered Felix. "Three to one."

"It was an ambush," said Crymea "They went right for Lady Flammare, that's how she was attacked."

"Flammare was attacked?" came the deep voice of Damiel Bartuas who materialized with a burst of flames next to Crymea. Everyone bowed when they spotted him, but his eyes were on his wife.

Damiel Enoch Bartuas looked angrier than Lex had ever seen. All seven-foot-tall of him was engulfed in a flame aura unique to the Bartuas Clan. The flames looked particularly menacing against his skin which looked like liquid dark chocolate. There were no imperfections, no weaknesses to exploit, he simply gave off an air of 'don't mess with me swagger.' With his flame aura in effect, he could perform the most powerful magick in his arsenal.

The watching Demimages took several steps back from him as respectfully as they could manage. His wife however, remained calm.

"Where is she?" he bellowed to the still struggling Felix.

"She's with the Healers," Storm answered for him.

"How did this happen? What was she doing out of the castle?"

"She was out on a recruiting mission," Nemfora answered and Damiel's eyes narrowed.

"You sent our daughter into enemy territory to recruit?" said Damiel slowly pronouncing every syllable like they were daggers.

"We all have our parts to play my love, Flame knew hers," said Nemfora, standing her ground. "The mission must be successful and for that we need more troops."

There was a moment when Damiel just stared at Nemfora then his red eyes went wide. Lex was certain that he and Damiel came to same conclusion. 'Nemfora planned this.'

"You knew something like this would happen. You were counting on it!" Damiel growled accusingly and with a wave of his hand, Felix was released and fell to the floor with a loud thud. "You used my daughter to be some kind of martyr?" The flames of his aura flickered dangerously.

This was unprecedented. Lex knew Nemfora was a cunning and ruthless witch, but never once had she put her own children into harm's way for GARGOYLE. Lex fought hard to hide his disgust as he gazed at the demon Queen. He looked around and saw all the eyes of the watching demons were on Damiel. If they found fault with Nemfora's actions, they too were hiding it.

"It was her idea dad," said Storm and Rain nodded.

"I don't care whose idea it was I should have been informed," he raged. As Nemfora's consort, Damiel was treated like a King. His business lay in armor and metal works, a profession made more volatile by the current war. He was not directly involved in sales or manufacturing, more the trading side of the business. Although he was a member of GARGOYLE, he rarely participated in their acts directly. He only provided the supplies necessary to the jobs done. His opinion on his children getting involved was illustrated that day. Lex wondered how Faith would react to the knowledge that her half-sister was out in Dorcela recruiting mages for Nemfora.

"She didn't tell you cause she knew you would worry," said Rain and he and his siblings tried to calm their father down.

"And who put her up to it?" he asked.

"Shall we discuss this more in private my love?" Nemfora suggested, noting the large audience their conversation had.

"Later," said Damiel in a low voice, then he turned to Storm, his expression softening. "I want to see Mare," he said, calling her by her nickname.

"I'll take you," said Storm rising from his seat.

"Let's all go see her," said Catlinis speaking for the first time since the meeting started and gesturing to her siblings. They nodded and one by one, they each disappeared in puffs of smoke.

"Crymea, Felix, return your quarters and await further instruction," said Nemfora. "That goes for the rest of you as well."

Lex thought Crymea and Felix's lives were spared thanks to Damiel's interference. Flammare's idea or not, it was their job to keep her from serious harm. He made to leave and relay everything to his own father and Faith when Nemfora called his name.

"Not you Prince Leafander, I want a word," she said, and she waited for the others to leave while Lex's mind reeled at the thought of being alone in a room with Nemfora. He would be in the perfect position to attack her. With a delicate flick of his wrist, his golden whip could be wrapped around her neck. Her death would mean his freedom. However, the idea of killing her disappeared from his mind as fast as he thought of it.

Destroying Nemfora would not destroy GARGOYLE. Any number of her children or followers would take her place. Catlinis was all but set up to rule. GARGOYLE would have to be dismantled in its entirety. Their entire way of life gone along with their will to fight. Then they could have peace and Lex could have his life back.

So, with Nemfora alone at her throne, Lex just knelt in front of her like Felix and Crymea did.

"You wish to speak with me your Grace?"

"Yes, tell me about Faith," she said leaning forward and speaking in a much lower tone than before. Lex, taken aback did not know what to make of her question. '*What exactly did she want to know?*' he wondered. "You're confused," she said when he did not answer right away.

"Forgive me, your question was unexpected."

"Then let me rephrase it. How are her powers progressing? Storm described her as impressive," she said with her finger tracing her bottom lip.

"That she is your Grace," said Lex. "The things she can do are impressive."

"Has she inherited any of my husband's abilities?"

"A fare few," he answered vaguely, not knowing how much he should divulge and how much Faith would want her worst enemy to know about her. Abilities among mages were unique to their bloodlines and knowing exactly what someone could do, was like knowing all the moves a fighter would use against you before you fought them. Lex could only confirm three of Nemfora abilities outright. The rest were only rumored about.

"I heard she can firefly," she said, her yellow eyes glowing.

"She can, I've seen it," said Lex said unable to hide his true feelings about it. He had only seen her do it once when he trained with her in the old campus but he would never forget the sight of her taking flight with a pair of fire wings on her back like some sort of half woman, half phoenix apparition. "It was a wonder to behold indeed," he commented.

Nemfora considered him for a moment then a closed expression appeared on her angular face.

"You've fallen for her haven't you?"

"I..." said Lex, flustered and inwardly chastising himself for being too truthful.

"It's alright," she said, throwing back her golden locks. "I expected it. Prince Leafander, I need her in GARGOYLE. I need her power and I will do anything to get it."

Translation, if Pride grew to have genuine feelings for Faith, it would be easier for him to lure her into the fold. But Lex had hide how he truly felt about Faith not just from Nemfora but from Damiel as well, who at the moment did not know of her plan.

"Are her abilities really necessary?" he asked as Pride. "Surely your Grace's own children..."

"My children have their talents," Nemfora started. "Catlinis is a great leader. She will serve me well with Cyphren at her side. But my other children did not inherit the bulk of Damiel's talents. Rain's strengths lie in diplomacy. Storm has no love for battle. Flammare inherited my ferocity and her father's brute strength but not many of the Bartuai High Fire abilities flourish in her."

'That's why,' said Lex to himself. The High Fire abilities were the most renowned in the magical world. High Fire was thought to be the most pure. Celestial Flame had more destructive power than any other flame in existence. It is the flame that made up Damiel's aura and Faith's wings.

"Lady Flammare could still develop it later," Lex argued, careful not to praise Faith too much. "Many powers come to fruition in later stages of growth."

"This is true," Nemfora commented but the way her eyes drooped told Lex that she was not convinced.

"Faith is developing them faster," she said, rubbing her delicate chin. "She is the daughter of a Star after all. Both her daughters could be potentials. The abilities they will inherit will far exceed any normal growth. Faith's destructive powers will awe all those who witness it. With her in GARGOYLE, nothing will stand in our way."

"Fear," Lex whispered before he could stop himself and Nemfora nodded with a wide grin across her pale visage.

"Yes, Pride, Fear. It is a powerful tool. The whole of Dorcela knows who she is and who she could possibly be. They would tremble and cower at her feet in the wake of what she will do for us. The power of a demon in the hands of a potential Star would shatter their entire belief system."

And there is was, Nemfora's true interest in Faith. Images of burned villages flashed across Lex's mind. His own village of Empyrean in ruins. And worst of all, the image of Faith flying through the sky throwing balls of flame the size of boulders. He fought hard to rid his mind of them. Lex knew his father Cloud had to be informed even if it meant more danger to Faith. If the Higher Order thought for a moment that Faith was a threat to public safety, they would either imprison her or destroy her.

12

A Disturbance

"I want happiness but at whose expense will I achieve it?" –
Anonymous

LEX DID NOT RETURN to Faith's apartment until late that evening when she was practicing her violin solo for the school musical. He appeared like a mirage through the mist at the edge of her bed. She smiled and poked him with her bow. With a huge sigh, he collapsed on the bed. Faith bit her lip. She was eager to find out what happened, but she did not want to press him especially seeing the mood he was in.

"What were you playing?" he asked

"My solo."

"Can you play it for me?"

Faith looked over at him with a wrinkled brow then she brought the violin back to the crook of her neck and played. Lex listened with a soft smile curving his lips lying motionless on the bed. Whatever happened at Nemfora's castle clearly had an effect on him and Faith hoped she could ease some of his anxiety with her music. Her fingers moved expertly on the strings having already memorized the music. She played until she could feel Lex drifting off to sleep, then she replaced her violin in the velvet lined box and joined him on the bed.

His arms slid from under his body to pull her close and Faith let him guide her into his embrace.

"Is everything okay?" she whispered against his body unable to keep quite any longer.

"Flammare was attacked while recruiting new troops," he said tragically, and Faith tensed as her hands came up to her mouth.

"Is she...?"

"She's fine, she will heal," he said calmly. "The injuries were only minor and there were no casualties."

"Why would they attack the recruiting, seems pretty counterintuitive if you ask me."

"How do you figure that?"

"The point of recruiting is to sow distrust among the people, to get them to hate the Higher Order and how they are running things right?"

"That's the gist of it."

"Then attacking the recruiting and injuring one of Nemfora's children would only serve to increase those beliefs. Innocents could have gotten hurt in that attack. What if GARGOYLE decided to take hostages?"

"Wow," said Lex staring at Faith unblinkingly.

"What?" she said exasperatedly hoping she did not say something stupid.

"You're absolutely right, that's exactly what Nemfora wanted," Lex explained and then he delved into the whole story, retelling the day's events including a very frightening description of her father Damiel and the anger he felt towards his wife. Faith pushed the image of her father engulfed in flames to the back of her mind thinking it was not something she wanted to deal with just yet. Then at the mention of her own name, Faith listened more intently.

"She's curious about me?" she asked, eyes wide. "Then our plan is falling into place."

"Yes, it seems that we've actually done it, we've fooled the most powerful mage of our age," said Lex excitedly but the way his eyes darted down and to the left made Faith ask another question. It was the first question that came to mind the moment he told her Flammare was attacked.

"Who was it that attacked the recruitment?"

"The Sister's Affinity."

Faith felt like she knew the answer before Lex had even spoken. *'How am I supposed to feel about this?'* she wondered. *'The group I used to belong to attacked my half-sister. My blood. I should feel enraged, but I actually feel hopeless. Stuck in the middle between knowing what was right and what was wrong. What can I do if anything?'* Then a thought came to her. Flammare might be beyond her help but Faith had another half-sister who needed her. Faith screwed up her courage to ask him an important question. Would Lex understand she thought, and better yet would he help her?

"Lex? I need a favour," she started, and he sat up in bed, pulling her with him so that they were facing each other.

"What is it?"

"I want to see Hope."

Whatever Lex's reaction to her request was, he kept it to himself because he did not respond physically or verbally, he just stared at her.

"I see," he said after a long moment with the same unreadable expression on his face. "What brought this on?"

"A feeling," she said desperately, twirling a curl between her fingers. "I need to know she's okay, does it make sense?"

"I am twin too remember, yes it makes sense," he said pulling Faith back into his arms and kissing her briefly on the lips. "We can go tomorrow after school if you have nothing on. It's a little late to go there now."

"Tomorrow would be perfect," said Faith after going over her schedule in her head and Lex squeezed her gently. She did not know what she hoped to accomplish by going to see her sister without Maurice's blessing, but she told herself she did not need it. Hope was her sister and he was not going to stop Faith from going to see her.

FAITH ARRIVED AT SCHOOL sans Pride for he was out with Cyphren getting in a morning feed before class. She spotted Saoirse with her face in phone near the front doors. Faith felt like she had not seen Saoirse in ages even though it had only been a week. She knew they had to keep their distance, but she did not factor in how much she would miss her best friend.

"Hey Soar," she said bumping into her shoulder and causing her to sway on the spot.

"Hi hun," her friend responded but her greeting lacked the normal brightness Faith was used to and it caused her to scrutinize Saoirse's face, looking for signs of weariness.

"You okay sweetie?" she asked warmly, her hand on Saoirse's arm.

"Huh, oh yeah, just had the longest weekend, sorry I couldn't help you move into your new place."

"Don't sweat it, you can come over anytime," Faith reassured her. 'Is that what was bothering her or is it something else?'

She kept looking at her phone and peering at the crowd of students in front of her.

"Who are you waiting on?"

"Catrianna and Mitch," she said pursing her lips.

"What? Why would they be toge...?" but then Faith froze when Mitch's car pulled up and she saw Catrianna practically float out of it with a flip of her hair. Mitch came around to her side where she was waiting for him, then they waked hand and in up to the school doors amidst stares and hearty sniggers from onlookers.

"Soar," Faith nearly growled and she grabbed hold of Saoirse's arm and dragged to a corner near a grouping of plants so Mitch and Catrianna would not see them.

"Explain that," she demanded, and Saoirse would not meet her eyes. She kept looking this way and that way with her head bowed.

"Well, you mentioned how we needed to protect Mitch, so he's been staying at Catrianna's house."

Faith blinked several times to make sure she had heard her friend right. Did she really just say that her ex-boyfriend and her frenemy were shacking up together?

"What the hell, why couldn't he stay with you?" she said fighting to keep her voice low.

"Okay my dad is cool, but he is not cool enough to let a grown man stay in our house," said Saoirse pointedly and Faith ran an agitated hand through her hair.

"So, what, they're all buddy buddy now, dropping her off at school? And why were her parents so blasé about it?"

"Pretty much, they hit it off the moment they met. You could practically see the sparks flying," said Saoirse with an exaggerated eye roll. "And Catrianna's dad and stepmother work with the Higher Order, hunting demons here on earth so they are really gun ho about protecting Mitch."

Faith's gaze drifted over the entrance courtyard to the pair who looked very comfortable next to each other. There was a familiar glint in Mitch's almond eyes that she only saw him give her and Faith felt a pang of jealousy. *What right have I to be jealous? I have Lex?'* she said in her mind, but Faith couldn't fight the urge to fling a ball flames to separate the pair who left very little space between them.

"He's being extra nice cause she got hurt in the raid over the weekend,"

"Wait! What, you guys were there in Dorcela?"

"Yep," she said holding her small head high. "The raid was planned for a while now."

"How did you know where they were going to be?" Faith asked curiously. From what she learned from Lex about the recruiting, they never visited the same place twice.

"A little clever investigating and the trick Caspian taught me about eavesdropping with water droplets," she said with a smirk. "We've noticed a pattern in their activities. They tend to go where there are known GARGOYLE sympathizers to help get some support. We had Mages at a number of places and got lucky. I wasn't in the village they raided unfortunately but Catrianna was, anyway, she clashed with the leader of their group and got a lot of burns. Took forever for Daia to heal them."

Faith listened with increased worry with each word she spoke. Saoirse was in deep with the Sisters Affinity. She was in Dorcela. She was trained enough to participate in a raid. They knew where GARGOYLE was going to be. But the biggest bombshell she dropped that she herself was probably unaware of was that Flammare had attacked Catrianna. Still processing the sheer amount of information, she received, Faith did not stop Saoirse when she approached the canoodling pair near the entrance doors.

"Come on Cat, the bell is going to ring soon," Saoirse groaned making them break apart immediately. It was amazing how intimidated the pair of them were at her considering that Saoirse was nearly a foot shorter than both of them.

Faith stayed in her corner off to the right, careful not to be seen by any of them. Feeling more distant from Saoirse than ever, she ran into the school building without a glance behind her. As she walked to her first class, she could not get what Saoirse revealed out of her head. The Sisters Affinity knew where they were recruiting so her siblings or even Pride could be hurt next. *'Should I tell him, or would that be betraying what my mother fought against just protect my boyfriend and my demon half siblings?'*

FAITH DID NOT SEE LEX until lunch that day, having skipped all his morning classes. She did not know if she was going to tell him what Saoirse let spill, so she put it out of her mind for the time being. She stood pouting next to her locker when he approached her. He swaggered up to her as Pride with Aubrey trailing behind him.

"You're late," she said, tapping her foot on the ground.

"I'll make it up to you," he said with a grin then he lifted her head with his index finger and gave her a peck on the lips before whispering. "Later." The students nearby did not even try to pretend they were not watching. Aubrey was the only one who looked away.

"To lunch we go," said Pride, throwing his arms about both hers and Aubrey's shoulders then they started down the hall to the cafeteria. Their table was as loud and lively as ever with Storm doing tricks with a couple of knives borrowed from other people's lunches. Thanks to the large crowd around their table, no onlookers could see.

"It's a shame Flame isn't here," Rain sulked as he made a grab for the knife Storm commandeered from him before wiping it profusely with a napkin so he could eat his meatloaf. "Not the same without her setting the knives a light."

Cyphren's eyes lingered over Faith at his words and she quickly looked away and busied herself with her meringue pie. After every second bite, she fed one bite to Pride who was in a heated discussion with Aubrey about attack formations in a sport Faith knew next to nothing about. Faith knew she was the reason Flammare had not enrolled in Alexander Prep along with her other siblings.

Rain hinted in a loud voice that she was not fond of the company they kept at school.

"You could light these couldn't you?" Storm whimpered leaning over to her with three knives wedged between his fingers like they were claws. "Rain and I would likely set our own hands on fire. Flame's the only one who could light them individually." Luckily, Faith did not need to demonstrate this because the bell sounded shortly after the words came out of his mouth.

"Maybe next time Storm," she said standing up with Pride and jamming a last piece of pie into his mouth. He smiled and kissed her full on the lips, sharing the tarty sweetness between them. It was an intimate kiss that she would rather have without an audience of demons and demon hangers-on; but she liked Pride's playful side. Lex was not nearly as playful as himself. Faith liked her brooding platinum blond boyfriend but sometimes she felt like she had two boyfriends the way Lex was with her at school.

The next couple of classes went by in blur. Faith was in Pride's arms for most of the lessons and never left her side since he was absent all morning. Faith could not hide her curiosity as she watched him in Math class that afternoon before study hall. The scent of decay that hovered around the demons in their circle was faint around Pride to the point of unnoticeable, but she knew he fed on a daily basis with Cyphren.

'How does he do it?' she pondered, her eyes on him instead of the math teacher. Faith had no desire to feed on humans but if there was a trick to fooling people into thinking she had succumbed, it could be used to her advantage but no matter how much she pressed Lex about how he fed, he would not divulge.

"It's no easy task," he explained one morning when they were practicing in the old campus, his face more serious than she ever saw on him. "Took your mother years to perfect it. One mistake and we will all be made."

'Aren't my powers developing faster than anyone could have imagined?' she argued in her own mind. *'Why wouldn't he at least tell me how it was done?'* She frowned in his general direction as Pride raised an eyebrow at her and nodded in the direction of the math teacher who Faith did not notice was standing in front of them.

"Miss Spiritwolfe, I told the class to take out their scientific calculators. Are you going to get yours or do you think you can calculate Co Sin on your own?"

"Sorry Mr. Granger, I'll get it now."

Face burning, Faith pulled the long device from the side pocket of her bag and got to work on the formula on the board. While she worked, she felt Pride slip a note into her lap. When he wrote it, she had no idea.

Still writing with her left hand, she opened the folded note with her right. In Lex's fancy script was the word; 'Rooftop.'

13

The Information

"Family. I thought I had it. Now it's gone and it won't come back." –
Anonymous

This time, it was Lex who waited for Faith to arrive at the rooftop that afternoon during study hall. He sat so erect Faith almost took him for a statue among the trees. He reached out for her with his slender fingers and guided her to spot next to him on the bench.

"Faith," he said tenderly, her hand still in his, lightly stroking her fingers. "There's something important I'd like to ask you."

"Oh?" said Faith scratching her head. "Cause there is something rather important I have to tell you."

"You first then, mine may be hard to follow."

"Alright then," she said her eyes squinting then she took a deep breath and said the next sentence very quickly. "The Sisters Affinity knew where GARGOYLE was going to recruit so they planted members there to attack them."

"What!"

Faith dove into a hasty explanation about was Saoirse revealed to her and he listened to every word she said with one hand to his mouth and one had still clutching hers

"Did they target Flammare specifically?" he asked, and Faith shook her head.

"It did not seem that way, but know that you say it, Catrianna would know what my sister looks like. I bet you anything she went for her after realizing who she was." Faith's lips involuntarily curved into a smirk as she imagined Flammare sending balls of flame Catrianna's way.

"I wouldn't put it past her," Lex agreed but she got as good as she gave according to eyewitness accounts."

"Flammare's pretty powerful isn't she?"

"She's the toughest of Nemfora's children," said Lex, his face hard. "Never backs down from a challenge or lets her weaknesses be known. She's as cunning and ruthless as her mother."

"Really? I would have thought Catlinis?"

"Catlinis doesn't sully her own hands, lets other people fight for her. Usually Cyphren who's a bit of a fool and likes to 'play' with his prey. He's a trickster, not a warrior. I would worry about Flammare more than any of her other children. You got me."

"I do," said Faith, chewing on her lip. The thought of facing any of her siblings in battle made her feel hollow. Enemy or not, they were part of her family albeit dysfunctional but still a part of her.

"Now are you ready to hear what I have to say?"

"Almost," said Faith turning to face Lex dead on. "I want you relay what I just said to Nemfora."

Lex blinked several times and studied her face carefully.

"Do you know what you're telling me to do?" he said slowly and in such a low voice Faith had to listen hard to hear his words. "It's treasonous."

"I want you tell your father too, but I think Nemfora and the others should know?"

"Why?" Lex asked frowning and staring at her like she had three heads.

"Because it works in our favour," Faith try to explain. The last thing she wanted was for Lex to think she was betraying them. "One, it garners trust from Nemfora while also limiting their recruitment options. Without a set place to go, they will have to go to places they will have fewer supporters and get less recruits."

Lex considered her for a moment, still studying her face with his scrutinizing eyes.

"You might have something there," he said frown fading. "I'll run it by my father. Hmm, do you read the Art of War in your spare time?"

"Just lots of sheet music," said Faith shrugging. "Now what is it you want to ask me?"

"Ah yes," he said, his eyes twinkling, and his hands returned to hers and held them up against his heart. Faith felt her own heart leap and her breath catch in her throat as Lex looked up at her with his dimpled smile. "Faith Ara Spiritwolfe, it would do me a great honor if you were to accompany me to my sister's wedding."

"Pileah's wedding? You want me there as your..."

"As my date. Officially as me, Prince Alexei Cloud Skye."

Faith gasped and almost pulling her hands away, but Lex held them firmly to his heart. She looked over at him, her eyes drooping.

"You want me to attend this wedding as Faith, as your date?"

"Yes," he said grinning broadly.

"When is it exactly?"

"That's just it, it's on your birthday, so you can stop dreading the day and spend it all with me."

"But wouldn't that be crazy risky? What about your father?"

"My father is aware that you and I keep company for the sake of my undercover work. You will only be there officially as Faith to my family. The other guest won't know who you are or be permitted to ask."

"Be permitted to ask?"

"Haha yeah, as the Crown Prince, who I court is none of the public's business. Things might be done differently in other monarchies you know, but on Dorcela our affairs so to speak are private and to ask about them is unacceptable."

"But won't they be curious?" Faith asked with a wrinkled brow, thinking of strangers eyeing her as she walked at his side.

"Of course, they'll be curious, I am the Prince," he said with a hearty chuckle. "They just can't ask and before you come up with another excuse to say no, your name is not as notorious as you seem to believe. The only people who the truth about your bloodline are members of the Higher Order, your siblings and the Spiritwolfe's."

"You mean to say that my birth isn't public knowledge even though I am daughter of a Star?" she said incredulity written over her lopsided face.

"They know Chryselda gave birth to two daughters, they don't know that they have two fathers."

"How do they explain us living apart?" Faith asked trying to find a hole somewhere.

"As the first born, Hope is given the title of Duchess. You are just Lady Spiritwolfe and you choose to live Off World like your mother before you."

"Wow," Faith exclaimed. "Got that sewn up pretty tightly haven't you."

"Yep," said Lex grinning. "So, will you come?"

"What about your duties as Pride Leafander?"

"Taken care of by the real Pride Leafander who already agreed."

Faith bit her lower lip and felt his heart beating fast beneath her fingers and looked into his adoring eyes and found that she could not refuse him this.

"Just one more thing," she said, and he gave her an exaggerated sigh. "I have nothing to wear to a royal wedding in Dorcela." Faith remembering the odd clothes she always saw him in.

"My other sister Selene has you covered, and she can't wait to dress you up. She and Pileah have different taste so she's looking forward to having someone to dress up in her clothes."

"Goodness, I have that to look forward to?"

"It'll be fine now will you put me out of my misery and say you'll come."

Faith leaned forward and kissed him full on the lips then pulled back and said. "It would be an honor my Prince."

14

The Duke of Dragonshire

I never felt more of an outsider than I did at that moment in that place. – Faith

After school, Faith and Lex returned to the rooftop, this time holding hands and facing each other.

"How exactly are we getting to Dragonshire? On dragon back?"

"No," said Lex with a chuckle. "But now that you mention dragons, they do roam freely there so try your best not to be too alarmed.

"Oh sure," said Faith rolling her eyes. "I'll just act like I see dragons all the time."

"They aren't that bad," said Lex frowning slightly "More like giant lizards that can breathe fire."

"Right," said Faith shaking her head.

"Two more things before we set off. One, I will appear as Pride to the people of Dragonshire and two I will glamour your clothing to look less like you're an Off-World school girl."

"Gee thanks, say what on earth is Off World? It's the second time you mentioned it?"

"It's what we call the human world," he explained, and Faith raised an eyebrow in disapproval.

"Makes me sound like an alien."

"To them you pretty much are but I will do my best to help you fit in."

"Sure."

"Now, close your eyes."

She did as he asked and felt her feet leave the ground. She shut them tightly and did not open them again until her felt solid ground beneath them.

Faith opened her eyes to a blinding light and shut them promptly before blinking several times as they adjusted. Once she could see again, her eyes opened wide and her jaw dropped at the stunning scene before her. Dragonshire looked like something out of fantasy game with hills and valleys as far as the eye can see. Two giant blinding suns hovering in the distance.

Miraculously, despite its large suns, the air was sweet and light and only slightly warm. There were islands in the sky supported by nothing but clouds and of course dragons the sizes of elephants laying on the fluffy grass or flying briskly through the sky. Their wings like the wings of a bat only larger and they behaved more like a heard of wildebeest than what Faith would have expected. When Lex told her that dragons roamed free in Hope's land she half thought he was kidding.

This was nothing like the infamous first visit to Resora with the Sisters Affinity. This was the real Dorcela in all its fantastical glory.

"What do you think?" Lex whispered in her ear.

"I have no words to describe this beautiful place that will do it the justice it deserves," said Faith breathlessly as she clung to Lex's arm and took in every sight her eyes could follow as Lex lead her through Hope's magical home. 'I can't believe she got to grow up here,' she thought while trying to hold back her jealousy.

As they made their way through a bustling cobbled village, Faith heard snatches of conversations full of unknown context. The men dressed a lot like Lex though she could tell his garb was more impressive. They wore tunics and pants made of some rough material and what looked like leather boots. The women wore long flowy dresses cinched at the waist either by design or with corsets. Faith pulled Lex even closer as a man in woman stared down at her very human looking clothing and muttered.

"Why can't visitors wear Dorcelian garb when they come here?"

"She's obviously from Off World, hope the children don't see her and think it's alright to dress like that."

Faith had half a mind to turn around, but she was pulled along by Lex who nudged her shoulder. She followed the direction of his sight and found herself once again speechless as they approached the tallest stone gate Faith had ever laid eyes on. It was a gate as tall as her 10-story apartment complex and flanked by two guards on dragon back. These dragons looked more menacing with black armor wrapped around their large bodies.

"State your business," chorused the guards at once.

"I am Prince Pride Leafander escorting Lady Faith Spiritwolfe."

The guards perked up as soon as they heard her name and put their shoulders back before pounding the large staves they held on to the ground. As they did, the gate that looked as solid as the ground she walked on, dissolved like it was made of liquid metal. They walked right through it and Faith watched it return to normal when they were on the other side and the foot of the long floating passage that lead up to what could only be Hope's home, the castle of Dragonshire.

It had towers and of varying heights and sizes. Every inch of the ground was covered in gorgeous trees filled with flowers Faith had never seen before. There were some that blew smoke, some that whistled when people passed and some that sparkled like live fairies were living inside them. Sitting atop the largest tower was a statue of a grand dragon standing tall with a crown made from what looked like every flower on the floating castle island. She and Lex approached the castle steps when a man in glittering robes glided down to them. It was not until the man was closer that Faith's squinting eyes finally recognize him.

"Uncle Malcom!"

"My dear Faith," he said extended a heavily jeweled hand to her. She almost ran into his arms until she felt Lex pull her back. Remembering herself, Faith straightened her face and shook his hand. It jangled like he was carrying a bag of coins. He looked a lot like Maurice with his blond hair and brown skin. Faith thought Maurice's hair was some odd recessive gene that made his eyes and hair light. His mother also had it. Faith often wondered why the gene skipped her, giving her only slightly fair hair. Malcom's children were completely blonde and curly haired. Now she knew the truth.

Faith looked up at him and the twin suns light caught his golden crown. "Do come in, there is much to discuss." He added with a nod as a dozen or so guards followed behind him. "Come, I will take you to my audience room."

Lex nodded and Faith followed him up the stone steps and into the castle. Faith paid no attention to the dazzling sights and sounds as Malcom Spiritwolfe lead them through his home. Her mind was on the stiff greeting she received. She met Maurice's brother several times including his very bratty son and daughter Kunela and Kriyon. Unlike Maurice, Malcom had always been warm and inviting during his visits. This new official Malcom was going to take some getting used to.

They were led into what looked like an old fashion sitting room fit for a Roman noble complete with a large tabled laden with baskets of fruit, bake goods, goblets of some red liquid and so many kinds of meat, he could open a deli.

Malcom gestured for them to take a seat at the table as he took his place at the head and grabbed the nearest goblet.

"Drink, I am sure you had a long journey from the village."

"Not terribly but I thank you Lord Malcom." said Lex as Price full of princely graces but he picked up a goblet just the same. Faith however just sat with her hands on her lap.

"Uncle Malcom, I am here to see my sister Hope," Faith announced without preamble, wanting to get the show on the road and skip the fake pleasantries. He obviously knew he was not her real uncle she surmised so he did not feel the need to be so familiar with her anymore now that she knew the truth. She only called him Uncle out of habit and the fact that they had an audience of about half a dozen servants who stood at the ready next to the guards that remained by Malcom's side.

"The Duchess of Dragonshire is currently unable to see guest. I wish you had sent word of your visit," he said quickly, eyes not meeting hers.

"Why?" Faith pressed not about to let the matter rest, not after traveling all the way here.

"Because I would have told you not to come," he said coldly, and Faith bit her lip.

"I meant why can't I see her?"

"She is indisposed," he said dismissively as he popped a grape into his mouth from the nearby basket. "Do try them, they are juicier than any grape Off World."

"To me or to everyone," snarled Faith, her face hard and Malcom finally met her eyes. He clenched his jaw and set the goblet down before clapping his hands loudly. The watching servants and guards disappeared in an instant.

"What did you? How did you?"

"I see we can do away with any royal sentiments now and speak like we used to," said Malcom leaning back in his chair.

"I don't know, can we? You were like a complete stranger to me before."

"Because I had to be, for the sake of appearances," he said.

"What appearances?"

"Public appearances. Servants talk," he said with a weary look on his regal face.

"So, what's going on, why can't I really see Hope?"

Lex straightened up and put down his goblet as he looked at her with his drooping eyes. She wanted to reach out the him, but they were on opposite sides of the table.

"Word has reached Dragonshire that you have been seen in the company of demons in Off World, the human world."

"And?"

"And as the Duchess of Dragonshire it wouldn't have been..."

"Prudent?" Lex finished for him with sneer.

"Let's go with that word."

Faith blinked several times and felt the anger swell up in her like a hot air balloon.

"So, I can't see my own sister because of what people would think? What am I an embarrassment to the Spiritwolfe name?"

"Nothing like that," said Malcolm holding up his hands. "I did not think you two should have been separated in the first place. You were legally adopted by my brother, both Off World and here. I still consider you my niece. But your sister has her future position to consider. As a beacon of light, she cannot associate with Demimages, even indirectly. Her light must remain pure.

"What does her being a Duchess have anything to do with this, she's not a Princess, it's not like she's going to rule Dragonshire," said Faith knowledgeably then she caught Lex's raised eyebrow and Malcom biting his inner lip. "Wait, you mentioned light and remaining pure," she said slowly. "She's not just a Duchess is she? She's a potential."

Malcom hung his head and did not speak but he did not have to. Faith knew it as soon as she thought it that it was true. Somewhere in the back of Faith's mind she wondered whether she or Hope could be potentials, but she did not dare ask Lex for fear of not hearing the answer she wanted. Blood relatives of Stars were often potentials just like her mother's aunt.

"So, Maurice is afraid I'll corrupt her with my demon blood?" scoffed Faith. "Where is he anyway?"

"On assignment for the Crown Prince who is another obstacle," said Malcom shaking his length of golden curls.

"The Crown Prince is Hope's cousin right, your nephew on your older brother's side?" Malcom and Maurice's older brother Markus never visited them. Maurice always argued he did not care for America, preferring to live abroad. Faith just did not know abroad meant an entirely different plane of existence or that he was the King of Dragonshire.

"GARGOYLE has made it known via our spies that they are trying to recruit the most powerful mages in Dorcela," said Malcom and Faith swallowed. "Currently...they have their eyes on Prince Vashaun."

Faith eyes darted to Lex's and back to Malcom. So, word had reached them of Nemfora's plans. Faith slammed her fist on the table and took several deep breaths before speaking again.

"And that is why you want me to stay away," said Faith evenly. "You think I'll lead Nemfora to Dragonshire?"

"What we think and what we hope to prevent," said Malcom and he clapped his hands and the guards from before appeared at once at his side, this time wielding sharp wide bladed weapons. "It's time for you to go dear niece."

Faith held back a sneer that she was able to turn into a painful smile.

"I daresay it is," said Lex rising from his seat and teleporting at Faith's side so fast she almost gave herself whiplash trying to follow his movements. He put a protective hand on her shoulder and guided her out of the dining room.

"Thank you for your humble hospitality Lord Malcom," said Lex courteously back in full Prince Leafander mode. "We will see ourselves back Off World."

He ushered her on and did not say a word to her until they were halfway down the floating platform that lead down to the dissolving gate. He stopped her when they were about 10 feet away from the bottom.

"How do you feel?" he asked tentatively, pulling her hand into his own and caressing her face.

"I don't know. Numb? My sister is a potential Star of Dorcela, and I am a demon spawn."

"You don't know you're not a potential too," Lex argued with a lopsided look, but Faith shook her head.

"You heard my Uncle. You must remain pure with your light untainted."

"You are!"

"I was born a demon, or did you forget? Born craving human energy."

"I'm sorry I..." he said hurriedly trying to pull her closer, but Faith took a step back from him.

"What? You meant now? Now that I am in knee deep with demons who want to recruit me. Yeah what a Star I'll make."

"Faith.."

"Can we not talk about this anymore? What's important is that Nemfora is targeting the Prince of Dragonshire in the hopes of corrupting him and maybe even Hope. Now I see why I need to stay away from her. We have to find a way to stop Nemfora's plan, somehow."

"That will be our next task," he reassured her, closing the gap between them, and squeezing her hand. "We won't let anything happen to your sister or the Prince."

Faith looked at the determined look in his beautiful eyes and the way his strong handheld hers with a firm grip and a gentle squeeze and she felt her tension melt away.

"Let's go home."

"Of course," said Lex making their way through the gate. Once they were safely on the other side and far enough away from the dragon rider guards, he wrapped his arms around her and teleporting them back to the Andromeda.

15

Poco a Poco

"Just when you think you can handle something, life reminds you it is not all that easy." - Faith

With the promise of finding a way to help Prince Vashaun and Hope, Lex and Faith strategized every chance they got. The problem was Faith found herself busier than she had ever been since moving to New York. Not only did she have finals to study for, the winter musical was fast approaching which meant many more rehearsals. Devonte and the rest of the cast had only two weeks to be completely off book. Faith beat out all the other violinist to become first chair which meant much more responsibility and pressure. She practiced well into the night most days, grateful for the soundproofed studio in her apartment. With the musical only 13 days away, Saoirse decided to throw Faith a housewarming party complete with games and New York's best pizza.

Lex was away on assignment as he had been for days. Faith was really looking forward to seeing Saoirse, so she rushed to the door when she heard the bell. Faith flung it wide open to great her friend and froze when she noticed Saoirse was not alone. Behind her were Devonte and Mitch, each carrying a box, one a large pizza the other what looked like a cake.

Saoirse flung her arms around Faith's neck startling her as the three of them pushed their way into her home.

"Oh, Faith I missed you so much," she screeched, still holding on to her as Faith shut the door behind them. The boys set the boxes on the kitchen counter and looked wide eyed around at her apartment. Faith was happy to see Devonte but looking at Mitch now brough the image of him and Catrianna. An image that made her insides writhe. She did not how to act around him now.

"I missed you too Soar," said Faith lightly, her hands on her friend's waist. "I missed...us." She added in a whisper.

"We are still us hun," said Saoirse releasing Faith's neck and linking arms with her.

"Are we?"

Faith thought about the past few weeks and the times they have spoken in person were countable on one hand.

"We're forever you and me," she reassured her. "We just have to work harder at keeping in touch, covertly is all."

"So, you haven't replaced me with Catrianna?"

"Replace you with Sparkles, heck no," said Saoirse throwing her head back.

"I brought Mario cart!" Devonte exclaimed, pulling out a game counsel from his backpack. "Thought we could do boys verses girls like old times."

"I'm down," said Faith feeling more carefree than she had in weeks as she joined the boys in the living room area and helped them set up the system.

"You get set up," said Saoirse gently pushing her towards the television. "I'll sort out the pizza."

"Deal."

"Winning team gets the most slices," Mitch declared with a lopsided grin and a crack of his knuckles.

"Also deal," said Faith with a soft punch on his shoulder. *I should at least make an effort to be friends with him. He did come here for me after all.*

"You know you haven't beaten me at Mario Cart since the 8th grade but whatever."

"Yeah cuz has mad skills," said Devonte shaking his head. "How about we rethink this bet."

"I've been practicing," Mitch defended himself while taking a seat on the sofa as Devonte hooked up all the controllers and handed him one.

"Let's see if it paid off," said Faith shrugging and taking the seat next to him on the sofa.

Saoirse joined them with pizza, plates, a liter of cola and a stack of cups.

"Let's get this party started!"

They played six rounds, the boys winning every other game.

"Aww we nearly had them in the last round," Saoirse moaned, throwing the controller down as the boys high fived each other.

"Best out of seven?" Faith challenged with a wide grin.

"You got it."

An hour later, the pizza was nearly all gone. Faith and Saoirse ate their extra slices with exaggerated noises and exclamations of its deliciousness at the boy's extent.

"You really have to do that huh?" said Devonte smacking his lips and looking hungrily at Faith's slice.

"Gotta savor the movement at retaining my undefeated status."

"So competitive," Mitch muttered.

"You know it."

"Let's eat cake!" said Devonte standing up and rubbing his hands together.

"Yeah," Saoirse agreed. "Losers can clean up the mess from the pizza."

"Don't add insult to injury!"

"I'll get the cake," said Mitch standing up and pushing Devonte back down into his seat. "Dev you clean up. Girls relax."

Faith watched him go to kitchen and a sudden idea struck her.

"Soar, can you help Dev? I'm gonna um..." Faith gestured in the direction of Mitch and mouthed the words. 'I wanna talk to him alone.'

Catching on, Saoirse gave her a quick nod and picked up her controller.

"Hey Vonte, let's play a round you and me?"

"Sure. Let's get it."

"I'm the Princess."

"As always."

"Oi!"

Faith walked slowly to the kitchen and watched Mitch carefully unbox the cherry cheesecake.

"Checking to see if I get cake all over your pristine counters?" Mitch accused when he caught sight of her.

"No, just wanted to see how you are, how you've been."

"You'd know if you picked up the phone once in a while, barely seen you since I've been here."

"I thought Saoirse explained why I have to keep my distance. It's dangerous. Plus..."

"Plus, what?" Mitch paused mid slicing the cake.

"Plus, I don't exactly get along with your new girlfriend."

"Ah," said Mitch and he continued cutting. "So, you know about us? Did Saoirse spill the beans?"

"She didn't have to, I saw you two together outside school," Faith explained, and Mitch did not look the list bit embarrassed in fact the grin on his face told her was happy she knew.

"Don't tell me, you don't approve?"

"It's not for me to approve, I just...don't know what you see in her."

"What do you mean?"

"She's short temped, standoffish and cold as ice."

"To me she's hot, she can be a bit chilly sometimes, but we clicked from the moment we met."

"Hot? Chilly? Are you describing a girl or a pepper?"

"Funny, we just hit it off okay, I was just saying to her in bed..."

"In bed?" Faith repeated, her eyes shooting to his. 'He can't mean...' She blinked several times and swallowed hard. "You two have already slept together?"

Mitch did not need to answer her. He scratched his temple like he always did when he was nervous, and Faith took a step back from him like suddenly he was radioactive.

"I can't believe you've already slept with her."

"What do you want me to say," Mitch questioned her. All the cake slices were sitting on individual plates, but he still had the knife in his hand. "There was an energy between us, we couldn't deny it and we both wanted it."

"So, all the time we were together you wanted something from me I wasn't ready to give you and you went and got it from some other girl after only a month or so of dating? What was I to you?"

"I loved you and I was willing to wait for you." said Mitch slamming the knife down but it did not stay down. Just like his temple scratching, things tended to float around Mitch when his temper was high. The knife hovered in the midair along with small things around the kitchen. "But you made it perfectly clear that we were over." The floating objects dropped to the ground as soon as he noticed them hovering near his head. "Maybe I should go. I shouldn't have come here."

"Maybe you're right," Faith snapped but she regretted the words as soon as they left her lips. He turned on his heal and made for the door. A stabbing in her heart made her call out to him. "Wait. Don't go."

"Why not?"

Faith bit her lip to stop her tears. He did not need to see them she told herself, but he needed to know why they would come.

"Because I've lost so much already this year, I can't lose you too," she said pleadingly, her lips trembling as she spoke. "I was out of line. Your love life is your business, not mine."

Mitch hesitated, his body leaning towards the exit. Faith knew that if she let him walk out of that door, there was a very real chance she would lose him forever but then he turned to face her.

"You writing a poem?"

"I mean it," said Faith. "I let my feelings about her get me all riled up. I don't want her to change us. We've been through too much together. I want you in my life Mitcham."

"I want to be in yours."

"Then we can put this behind us?"

"We can."

Mitch snapped his fingers and the plates of cake lifted up and followed him out into the living room. Faith watched them go but did not join him just then. She leaned against the counter and put her hand to the pendant around her neck and squeezed it tightly.

"Lex, come back soon," she whispered knowing he would he hear her.

16

Scherzo

"I know what I have to do, I am just afraid to do it." - Anonymous

Lex knelt in front of Nemfora's throne as Pride with Cypren and Aubrey on either side of him. Nemfora was sitting with her legs crossed and her blue eyes narrowed in his direction. Storm, Flammare and Rain were sitting at their own thrones. Flammare barely acknowledged Pride's presence. Since she found out he was keeping company with Faith, as far as she was concerned, he was dead to her. The rest of their siblings were away or in the human world. Damiel was sitting at his wife's side.

"I've come to bring some news," he prefaced. "News I think will interest you both greatly." He nodded to Nemfora and Damiel in turn.

"Yes, my son tells me Faith brought something to your attention," said Nemfora at the mention of Faith, her eyes darted to her husband and then back to Pride.

"Yes, she obtained this information from a member of the Affinity that they've been monitoring our recruitment activities."

"To what end?"

"To ascertain a pattern."

"But you never recruit in the same place twice," said Damiel to his wife who nodded curly.

"Yes, but a pattern did emerge," said Pride.

"How can that be!"

"We routinely conduct recruitment activities in places with GARGOYLE sympathizers. Known ones and they caught on. They might have even planted fake ones to draw us in."

"And that's how Mare was attacked!" said Rain banging his fist on his armchair.

"It could be," said Pride, his brows knitted.

"Those sneaky little witches," Nemfora exclaimed but more calmly than her son. Damiel fixed Pride with a scrutinizing stare.

"Why did she tell you this?" he asked Pride, eyes unblinking.

"To be honest I am unsure of her motives," said Pride and something of Lex's own doubts registered on his face. He heard Faith's explanation, but something told him that was not the full story. He knew Faith too well, probably more than she knew and he had a pretty shrewd idea why she divulged but he was careful to leave that out of his explanation to his father. "Faith heard what happened to Lady Flammare and it is my belief that she might have been worried something like that would happen again."

Flammare scoffed in his general direction. Rain mimicked her. Damiel was unreadable but Nemfora was thoughtful.

"Why would she care?" said Flammare with a sneer, her dark eyes still not looking at Pride.

"She cares enough," said Storm, putting his hand on top of hers but she snatched it away. "After all she is our sister."

"I'm your sister! She's nothing! She's not one of us and she never will be!" Flammare disappeared leaving only embers in her seat. Nemfora glanced at the burning embers and then addressed the room at large.

"It might have been a mistake to let her know of our plans," she said, throwing back her head.

"She had a right to know," Rain argued, and he too disappeared.

"I'll speak to her," said Nemfora rising from her seat. She took two steps before pausing in front of Pride. "You've done well Prince. You've gained her trust and mine."

She lightly brushed her hand across his head in what was supposed to be an affectionate way and Lex fought hard not to recoil at her touch. Then she floated away and out of sight.

"Do you really think she did it cause she cares about what happens to us?" Cyphren now asked as Pride got to his feet.

"She does," said Storm confidently, a broad smile on his boyish face. "You guys forget, I spend the most time with her besides Pride. She is genuinely interested in getting to know us and our ways and I don't know, she's fun, I like her. I want her here with us, where she belongs. Don't you dad?"

Damiel did not answer. Nemfora only informed him of their plan recently and Lex was not privy to his reaction. But Cypren did mention a lot of raised voices ending in Damiel leaving the castle for a number of hours. Lex wanted to know how he felt about Faith as much for as for their cause. Lex knew that really wanted to know her father. It was not a sentiment Lex shared so he could not sympathize. Thinking of his relationship with his own father that raised him, he was lucky to get a civil word from him these days.

"What I want," Damiel started and then he paused, his lips tight. "What I want does not matter. If Faith wants to be here, then she is welcome." He signaled to Storm and they were gone in a puff of smoke. Lex did not know what to make of Damiel's pronouncement, but one thing was for sure, Faith's plan was working.

17

Moon Sister

"I never felt more at home than I do here." - Faith

F aith stood in front of the full-length mirror in Selene's vanity and studied her appearance. She thought she looked like herself just a little more done up than she was used to. Selene was exactly like Faith imagined her, loud, friendly and the splitting image of her brother, even down the platinum blond hair. But her features were softer and youthful, but she was tall with the grace of a ballet dancer.

Selene stood behind her, teasing her hair and Faith could not help staring at her. Yes, she looked like Lex but there was something about the way she carried herself and the faint glow of her skin that made Faith mesmerized by her. Like the fun sister, she always dreamed of having who would let her borrow her clothes and try her makeup except in this case, make up was a glamour done by magic. Faith had only seen Lex do a few practical spells. The only spells her taught her had to do with fighting.

"Where do you learn all, this make up magic?" Faith asked as Selene twirled her fingers to curl Faith's lashes. "Is there some kind of makeup beauty school?"

Selene laughed and it was a beautiful controlled laugh that made her whole face glow.

"There is a school though not specifically for beauty," she answered. "Every kingdom in Dorcela has their own and they're all immensely proud and extremely competitive. I studied under the Grand Master Astra at the Empyrion School for Girls."

"Wow," whispered Faith thinking of the fictional all girl magic school with the pupil who made a lot of trouble and was thought to be a bad witch but always had her heart in the right place. Then her thoughts drifted to her mother. She never mentioned her schooling in her diary.

"Did my mother attend school there?" Faith asked forcing herself not to chew her lip so she would not mess up her lipstick, but she would not stop wringing her hands.

"She did," said Selene with a wink. "And she was famous. Got into so much trouble with her wild friends until she was snatched away to a speacial school for potentials and then she became legendary." Selene's eyes sparkled and Faith was eager to hear more but then there was a knock at the door that halted their conversation.

A woman dazzlingly beautiful glided in as if on skates. Faith sat up straight the moment she caught sight of the crown on her head that looked like it was made from shards of crystal. Every inch of it covered in white diamonds, almost as white as her hair. Faith could see her son in her soft features and her light eyes but also in her dimpled smile. Faith thought the Queen of Empyrion would be more intimidating but her dainty smile and short stride had a relaxing effect on Faith. The servant girl Tilly dropped to a deep curtsy and Faith wondered if she should do the same.

"Greetings, dear Faith, I so wanted to meet you before you came downstairs," she said in a breathy voice and her eyes fixed on Faith. She made to stand up and greet Lex's mother properly, but the Queen held up her hands. "Oh, don't stand on my account dear, you'll wrinkle your dress."

"And put me in a right state," Selene added from behind her. She found Faith's eyes in the mirror and extended a hand to the Queen. "May I present my mother, Queen Amirah, Light of Empyrion."

"I'm delighted to finally meet you your Grace," said Faith lowering her head in a bow and grateful she remembered from Lex how to address his mother.

"The delight is surely upon me my dear. I've been dying to meet you. To think your birthday would fall on the day of my eldest daughter's wedding. I hope you do not feel odd celebrating your birthday with strangers. Alexei told the staff what your favourite desserts are we will try to replicate them as closely as possible to make you feel more comfortable. Sweets always make me happy." said the Queen and she looked it with her eyes twinkling and her hands at her face.

"Please do not worry yourself on my account your Grace, this is exactly where I want to be on my birthday," said Faith truthfully. It saved her from imagining the grand ball her sister was probably having and from crying herself to sleep alone because Lex would still have traveled to Dorcela.

"Oh, you look so much like your mother," said the Queen gushing and pulling Faith out of her dark thoughts.

"Do I?"

"Oh yes and not just in the hair oh and Alexei tells me you inherited some of her gifts as well. We don't often hear from him but when we do, all he talks about is you."

Faith felt her cheeks burn as the Queen laughed, her eyes full of appraisal.

"Mother, you're embarrassing her," Selene chided.

"Am I dear?" she asked, putting a light hand on Faith's shoulder. The place where she touched her skin felt warm and soothing, like she was somehow sending her a calming energy through her palm, but Faith did not know that kind of magic was even possible. All her embarrassment from before seemed to be washed away leaving a wonderful sensation in its place.

"How did you...?"

"Mom was a potential," said Selene quickly who obviously understood what her mother did. "She has the power to heal the mind."

"Of some ailments," the Queen corrected her with a nod. Then she bent down so that she was at eye level with Faith and Faith froze, still dazzled by her beauty. Her hands came up to cup Faith's face in her hands like she was holding a delicate piece of porcelain. "Dorcela is ready for you Faith Spiritwolfe and don't be nervous, this is your true home and when everyone sees you downstairs, they will welcome you back with open arms." Her warm hands slid from Faith's face then she tapped her on the nose, then glided out the door.

Faith stared after her for a long moment after she was gone. Her thoughts were a jumble and completely incoherent. She thought of the reception she would receive when she came down and the questions they would ask. Lex coached her on the ones she was mostly likely to get. 'But will I ever be truly prepared?' she pondered as Selene got back to work on fixing her up do.

"Sorry about my mother, she's a lot to take," said Selene with a painted smile.

"I thought your mother was exquisite," breathed Faith, the warmth of her hands still lingered on her face. It was a mother's touch. A touch Faith had never really known.

"You really thought so huh? Well she took to you immediately."

"Does Lex, I'm sorry Prince Alexei really talk about me?" Faith asked, looking up at Selene's reflection in the vanity mirror and a wide smile formed.

"You can call him Lex when we are in private," Selene encouraged with a nudge in her back. "And yes, he does. A lot."

"And you..." Faith paused. Out of all the reasons she was nervous about being there with Lex, what she asked next was the biggest deterrent. "And you don't think it's odd for him to be with me. Given how much older he is?"

Selene looked around and gave a curt nod to Tilly who dissolved into wisps of smoke drifted out the window.

"Okay Faith let me stop you right there," said Selene holding a hand up. "Human perception of age should not be taken into account. Dorcelians age a lot slower. Time moves very slowly here. We do not measure time in years. We measure moon cycles."

"What does that mean exactly? How old is he?"

"Let me put it to you like this," Selene started as she dusted Faith's curls with what looked like powdered gold. "Your mother had you when she was still an adolescent in the eyes of our people."

"Yes, Lex told me that."

"But I don't he got it through to you," Selene surmised with a raised eyebrow. "When I say adolescent, I mean your mother was practically a teen mom. Her pregnancy shocked the Kingdom."

Faith gaped at Selene like a goldfish.

"No? For real?"

"Lex and Pileah are a little younger than your mother. Many human years have passed since your birth, but that time was insignificant here. Lex and Pileah had one birthday since you left here at one years old. You and Hope aged normally Off World because time moves so differently there. You lived with your uncle and aunt in California, she lived with your grandparents in Florida until she came of age. When she came into her powers and it was known she was a potential, Maurice sent her to school here. The Celestial energy in both of you had to mature faster to protect you in the human world."

Quantum physics was not exactly Faith's forte. She had to know in the simplest of terms.

"So, if you were to put Lex's age in Off World years, how old would he be to me?" Selene looked up, her finger to her chin then she looked back down at Faith.

"19 years old. His next birth celebration is in about a hundred celestial cycles. You'll be 18 then."

"And he'll be 20?"

"And how old are you? If it's not too rude to ask," Faith added hastily but Selene was smiling.

"I would be 15, everyone here still treats me like a kid," she sighed, rolling her eyes.

"Which would also make Pileah a teen bride," said Faith remembering that she and Lex were twins.

"Haha yeah."

"And your family is totally okay with that?" Faith asked, frowning as she recalled grimly Lex's ill-fated marriage to Faye and Selene's eyes suddenly darted down and to the left.

"Well Pileah can pretty much do whatever she wants around here after uh."

"After what happened with...her powers," said Faith regretting even mentioning it now and grateful she remembered Lordona's name was not to be mentioned in their household. She could tell how unformattable the topic made Selene. Lordona was also her sister and she turned on Pileah and tried to destroy her. "So, Lex and Pileah are about 2 Off World years older than me?"

"That's right and about as simple as I could explain the whole age thing," said Selene with a sigh, clearly happy to be done with the topic. Tilly returned silently at Selene's side holding a wooden box.

Faith could not help but feel relieved as well and she smiled at her own reflection. A reflection that was quickly changing thanks to Selene's efforts.

"This is a lot of gold," Faith remarked, looking down at her golden dress, the flecks of gold on her eyes and the powder in her hair that made the mountain of curls on top of her head held together by a lattice crown and magic.

"You're right," said Selene and with a flick or her wrist, light red eyeshadow appeared on her eyelids.

"Now for the finishing touch." Selene magicked the wooden box from Tilly's arms and out she pulled a bracelet that looked like it was made of molten lava. The bracelet itself was coils of flames held together by red chains that fit around her middle finger. It went perfectly with the flame ring. Like they were made to be worn together.

"That's gorgeous," Faith exclaimed unable to take her eyes off it. She could have sworn that the flames even flickered for a moment when she looked at them in the light.

"It's yours," said Selene with a wink. "Happy 17th birthday."

"I don't know what to say," Faith whispered, her eyes still on the flames on her wrist. "I love it, thank you so much Selene."

"Thank you for putting a smile on my big brother's face," whispered Selene in Faith's ear and once again she felt herself going red in the face.

"I didn't. I couldn't."

"You did," she said still more quietly probably because of Tilly. "My brother has been miserable since the day Chryselda died and before she came into his life for reasons I am sure you are aware of. But your presence in his life seemed to have an amazing effect on him."

"Really?"

"Truly and before you go doubting me," Selene added. "You are the first and only girl he has ever brought home to meet his family. "The look on his face when he talks about you...oh if only you could see. He adores you Faith. I know it."

She did not say anything but look down at the flames on her wrist once more. Lex' affection for her was felt but never declared but Faith's knew how she felt and hearing his family talk about him only solidified her feelings for him.

"You ready for your big entrance Faith?"

"As ready as I will ever be," said Faith trying to stand up in the 4-inch heels Selene let her borrow. 'Should have practiced walking in heels again,' she chided herself. She had not worn heels since she left California thinking she had no use for them in a uniform school.

"Lex will be downstairs already," Selene informed her while bouncing on the balls of her feet and grinning expectantly. Faith got the idea she was eager to see Lex's reaction to her look and Faith had to admit, she wanted to see it too.

18

Love Story

"Standing there with her in my arms surrounded by my family, I realized something important, that it felt natural and it was beautiful."

- Lex

LEX NEVER THOUGHT HE would find himself surrounded by members of the Empyrion court again and with their whispering and snide remarks, he was grateful it would not be a regular occurrence. He fidgeted this way and that way in the grand ball room, eyes looking up at the staircase every free moment he had. Conversations went over his head, but he honestly did not care. He was not there for them.

Dorcelian weddings were a drag as far as Lex was concerned, leaning back in his seat at the high table. His father's seat was noticeably empty. The Scepter dressed head to toe in white robes that concealed his face and the current Star of Dorcela took their presiding positions standing behind in the middle of the high table.

When the Star caught sight of Lex slumping in his seat, she wagged her jeweled finger at him, and he sat up straight with a smirk in her direction. Taea Ilba was 100 moon cycles younger than Chryselda when she took over as the Star.

As the older potential, the position was forced on her and Lex gave her all the he could after the time he spent with Chryselda in her early years. Eyeing Taea now, he thought she suited the position well. She greeted everyone who passed cordially with a warm smile. All of them

117

bowing and most trying not to make eye contact with her, for fear of her reading their thoughts.

Lex stared boldly into her emerald eyes and Taea raised her neat eyebrow at him in turn. She mouthed the words,

"You're planning to slip away after my blessing aren't you?"

He gave her the tiniest of nods back and thought. "You'll cover for me won't you?" Shooting her his best puppy dog eyes and she looked away with a slight tinge of pink on her cheeks.

"You think you are so charming don't you?" she mouthed.

"I know I am."

"I'll do what I can so you can slip away your birthday girl," Taea mouthed after greeting another guest.

"Thank you Tae," he whispered with a wink and she just rolled her eyes.

There was a loud thud and a collection of gasps from somewhere above them and Lex stood up expectantly.

There at the top of the stairs was his little sister Selene next to a vision of beauty. Lex's mouth fell open as he followed Faith's procession down the marbled staircase taking in her silky golden dress and the way it hugged her womanly curves. Lex did not know if it was magic or Faith, but she seemed to practically glow with a golden hue. Her angular face found his and her crimson lips curved into a smile. Eyes followed her every move until she was right in front of him and the guest had to politely pretend they were not staring.

His sister said something to him, but her voice was strangely muffled like his ears were plugged with algae.

"Alexei!"

"Huh?" he said finally looking away from Faith to stare at his sister who was clicking her teeth. "Sorry Lena oh and thank you."

"You're welcome," she said with a swift kiss on his cheek then she left to greet Taea leaving Faith standing before him looking like a goddess.

"Do I clean up alright?" said Faith a smile forming in the corner of her lips.

"You clean up very nicely my lady," said Lex planting a warm kiss on her hand then he guided her to the seat beside him. His mother and father finally took their seats next to the groom's parents and the Scepter gave the signal to begin the ceremony.

In true Dorcelian wedding fashion, the tables made a square in the middle of the ball room leaving space in the middle for the wedding circle. Pileah's wedding circle was gold like the theme for the wedding and painted into the ground with celestial symbols, protective spells and blessings. Lex commented inwardly that it looked like a mix between a map of the stars and a clock dial, so very Dorcelian.

The Scepter clapped his hands and the room was plunged into darkness with only the wedding circle lit on the ground. The stars and constellations moved clockwise around the circle and then Taea began to chant in the ancient scholarly tongue and a magical mist erupted from the ground to form a huge arch. With one last chant, a burst of light emitted from the top of the arch and Pileah and her husband to be Calum appeared beneath the arch to an applause filled with gasps and awes.

"Are all weddings here like this?" Faith whispered in his ear. Lex reached across her lap and pulled her hand into his own, answering her question with a squeeze. One squeeze yes, two squeezes no. A form of communication they came up with for their undercover work.

Pileah looked stunning in a wedding gown that looked like it was made from light and magic. It was white and gold and made her look like a bejeweled swan. Lex could not help but swell with pride as he gazed upon her. Taea walked around and blessed the circle but his eyes were on his sister. Even in the semi darkness, Pileah's eyes found his and they were filled with love. His heart ached for her, his twin. His other half. They were once as inseparable as Cyphren and Catlinis. Then both of their lives were torn asunder by people they loved and thought loved them.

"Oh Pi," he whispered too silently for anyone to hear but looking at her tiny nod, he felt she did.

Taea recited her final blessing and then the happy couple were released from their arched cocoon and the guest applauded once more with Pileah grinning broadly in the middle of her circle.

"Presenting for the first time, Her Royal Highness Princess Pileah Claribel Skye Brigham and the Honorable Prince Calum Brigham!" the Scepter announced. The main lights came back on, but the circle still shimmered, waiting for their first dance as a married couple. Music sounded from the orchestra situated on an inner balcony. Pileah and Calum danced within the circle as tiny orbs of light danced around them. After a few moments, Taea signaled for others to join them. Lex stood up at once and bowed to Faith, still grasping her hand.

"My I have this dance me lady?" he asked, and Faith lip twitched, no doubt she wanted to laugh but she just cleared her throat and grinned.

"Yes, you may."

He guided her to the dance floor and owning to that fact that Faith was unfamiliar with Empyrion court dances, only did a waltz with her. Thankfully, it matched the music. Other couples performed traditional dances around the wedding circle with the bride and groom in the middle. Upon passing by Pileah, Lex leaned towards her.

"Congratulations Pi," he said brightly.

"Congratulations your Highness," said Faith inclining her head in a slight bow which Lex noted.

"Thank you both very much," said Pileah her voice more high pitched than he was used to, no doubt because of how happy she was. "And it's so good to meet you Faith Spiritwolfe. You two look lovely together. Don't the Cal?"

Her husband Calum just grinned and nodded, going a bit red in the face. *'Poor guy is still nervous around me,'* he said in his head, fighting to keep the smile on his face. Some of his mirth was visible to Pileah who gave him a stern look. Not wanting to hog the new couple, Lex waltzed Faith over to the far right where there were few couples and they could talk freely.

"Have I told you how incredibly gorgeous you look tonight?" he whispered in her ear and felt her shiver in his arms.

"Have I told you how handsome you look?" she said as she flicked the string of diamonds dangling from his pierced ear. "Is it weird I want to borrow your earring?"

"It's an Empyrion traditional earring," Lex explained, holding her a bit closer and she put her head on his shoulder. "Noblemen wear them to important events."

"Did your sister put any traditional Empyrion jewelry on me?"

Lex slipped his hand down the length of her arm and fingered the flame bracelet on her wrist.

"This bracelet," said Lex. "Worn to ward off evil deities. Forged by Celestial Flame and by the highest of noblewomen. It's extremely powerful."

"Woah, she didn't tell me that," said Faith, her body going tense for a moment. "I will definitely take good care of it."

"I have no doubt that you will. Might come in handy someday," he added with a small kiss on her shoulder then he scanned the area until her found Taea chatting with his mother. He gave her a small nudge in her mind, and she turned to look at him. Her fingers made the number 2 and he understood immediately. *'Thank you Tae. I owe you.'*

"Right, in two minutes we are going to slip away," he murmured close to Faith's ear.

"Why?"

"Do you really want to engage in small talk with my nosy relatives gawking at you?"

"Uh definitely not."

"Then hold on to me and don't say a word."

The seconds ticked away so slowly Lex felt like time was slowing on purpose and then finally he saw Taea give him the signal and then he and Faith dissolved into floor beneath them unseen by anyone. They appeared in his empty apartments some 300 meters away from ball room and many flights of stairs up. Still holding Faith, he squeezed her waist and she squirmed away and then stared around at his room.

He watched her wide eyes taken in everything from the high ceilings, to his glass chest of crown jewels and the many portraits that papered the walls. Portraits of him and the princes who stayed there before him. Then her quizzical gaze found the ajar door to the balcony right where he wanted to lead her. Watching her and following her slightly, she slipped through the door and leaned against the banister as all of Empyrion was lit below her. It looked just as he left it. Loud, boisterous, and full of light. Lamps lit by magical mist. White winged horses pulling carriages, fountains of blue and purple water and fairies flying hither and dither.

Lex joined her on the balcony and slipped his arms around her waist in a back hug enjoying her warmth. Her head fell back upon his chest and it felt good to be home in Empyrion with her.

"This is what I wanted to show you. How do you like my town?"

"I love it, your home is beautiful." she exclaimed in a breathy voice.

"More beautiful than Dragonshire?"

"Definitely. The town, the people, the fashion, your family. Everyone is so inviting. I feel good here."

"You know this was once your home too? You were born here."

"I was?"

"Yes," he said and her turned her in his arms until he was facing her, and she was leaning against the balcony wall. Lex was thankfully it was magically enclosed for security. They could see out, but no one could see in. "You belong here and maybe one day this will be your home again."

"Live here in Dorcela?" she said, brows furrowed.

"I know you want to attend a music school but that won't be for long. Once this business with Nemfora is over, I can come back, with you. You can study magic and learn about where you came from." said Lex. He wanted her to call this place her home again when he was safe to really to return to it himself. Lex could not imagine being back there without her. He knew it to be true. All the time he spent away from her in Dorcela, running errands for GARGOYLE, all he thought about was how he was doing it for her when before it was just to be with his family again. He knew what had triggered the change and he wanted her to know it too.

"Faith, what keeps me going, what makes working for Nemfora bearable is knowing I have you to come back to whenever I am away."

"Oh Lex."

"Let me finish," he said, and she nodded with a bite of her lower lip. 'She is not making this easy.' Seeing her illuminated against the blanket of Dorcelian stars just made him want her more and want to tell her what he had been feeling for months now. "Our relationship may have started quickly, but what I've been feeling about you developed over time. With each passing day, you began to mean more and more to me, and I know why. It's because I love you."

Faith stood perfectly still as her eyes glistened and filled with tears. 'Oh no, had I said it too soon. Did I startle her?' He took one panicky step towards her and she flung her arms about his neck

"Faith?"

She pulled back slightly and planted a wet kiss on his nose.

"I love you too," she said and her held her tight and spun her around the balcony unable to hide his glee. Then he set her down on the ground and kissed her warmly on the lips.

"I love you so much Faith, I was made to love you. I know it."

"I know it...too," she said with a corner smile and she took a few steps back from him and he gave her a crooked look.

"What do you mean?"

"Lex, have I ever told you I sometimes have visions or feelings I can't explain?"

"Yes," said Lex slowly, taking in every word.

"I had a vision the first time we kissed, and I thought I was seeing someone else, but it was me and you. And before you and I met, I had a vision in Orchestra class. I think my mom sent me a vision of the past cause in it she was talking to you in a meadow. She was going on about life in a cage and you mentioned how you'd never..."

"How I'd never find love again," said Lex, the words came out of it his mouth like he had spoken them yesterday and not many moon cycles ago and then his eyes met Faith's and he understood. He knew remembered what Chryselda told him that day and he felt tears sting his eyes before he could stop them.

"My mom told you that she didn't believe you, that she knew you would love again. She said she did not know how but she knew it to be true. She sent me that vision because..."

"Because she saw you," said Lex looking up and blinking the tears away. "She saw our future. She saw us. Oh Selly."

"That's what you called her in my vision," said Faith, her tears flowing freely. "And she called you.."

"AC."

"Which stood for, Alexei Cloud."

Faith reached out to him and he grasped her hand and pulled into a kiss. Her tears on her face, her tears on his. Tears for the person who brought them together. Tears for the love they knew was real. Lex wrapped his arms around her waist and pulled her back into the apartment and magicked the balcony door shut behind them. Their lips still entwined, he led her across his apartment and set her down on the winged sofa next to the fireplace.

He kissed her softly at first, enjoying the warmth of her mouth and the sensation of her hands on his waist, fingers pulling at the fabric until she was touching his bare back. Then his slipped his tongue into her sweet mouth and felt her squirm beneath him and her moan vibrate against his lips. Then his lips left hers to trial kisses down her neck and she moaned more deeply. He stopped briefly to look at her beautiful face and found her eyes full of affection for him.

"Faith, I don't know if I can control what I am feeling right now, if you wish to return downstairs we can," he did not wish to push her further than she was willing to go but then she kissed his collarbone and he had to fight his instincts. "Faith?"

"Lex, I am exactly where I want to be, here with you," she said breathily. Lex beamed at her and captured her lips once more in a passionate kiss. Many moments later, he would lead her to his bedroom.

19

Spy

"It's the people closest to you that can cause the most harm." -
Anonymous

Faith woke up many hours later in her own bed in the
Andromeda. It took her a moment to remember why she was so
happy. Why the day seemed brighter, why the air felt lighter and why
she could not stop smiling. Then she looked to her right and saw Lex
laying asleep beside her, bare backed and sleepy faced. His hand came
up and brushed the strands of her once neat hair now a curly mess, her
behind her ear.

"When did we come back here again?" she asked, cocking her head
to the side as she racked her brain for the memory.

"When your stomach started growling," said Lex sitting up. "I
magicked some food from the wedding here. We ate and then you fell
asleep."

"Wow last night was a blur," she said pulling her hair into a
ponytail, so it was out of her face.

"All of it?"

"Not...all of it," said Faith in a small voice then she kissed his bare
shoulder.

"Should we have breakfast?" he suggested, returning the shoulder
kiss.

"We should get dressed and cleaned up first," said Faith looking up
at his messy hair. It looked like tangled up clouds.

"Right!"

An hour later they were sitting at the counter, eating leftover grilled
chicken, mashed potatoes, and wedding cake. She fed him a spoon full

of pudding and he fed her bits of the lemon drizzle cake in between kisses. Faith felt like they were the newlyweds. Then Lex slapped a hand to his head, starling Faith who had a spoon full of pudding in her hand.

"Lex, what's the deal?"

"I forgot your birthday presents," he said, his reddening forehead in his hand.

"Its fine, you know I'm not big on birthdays," she commented trying to keep the memories of past miserable birthdays at bay as she hovered the pudding in front of his face. He ate it and then dissolved into whips before her eyes leaving her stunned, still holding the now empty spoon. Frowning, she was about to drop it into the pudding bowl but then he reappeared at her side with an arm full of boxes.

"What's all that?"

"Well I asked around, saw a few of your relatives and old acquaintances of your mother if they could get somethings for you."

"You didn't have to do all that," she said, setting the spoon down and giving him a hand with the boxes.

"I wanted to make your birthday special."

"You already did that," she added, not meeting his gaze for fear of her face burning.

"Well extra special, come and open them."

Feeling like a child at Christmas, Faith dropped to the floor with Lex and opened the first box. Inside was a magical music box that played the song from the wedding, complete with a miniature figurine couple dancing in the middle like Pileah and Calum did. The next box held books of magical spells, blessings, and enchantments. Faith was eager to dig into those and start looking for glamour spells.

"Open this one next," said Lex, handing her a large box wrapped in white. "It's from your aunt."

"Lucia? Mom's sister?"

"Yep."

Faith's eyes widened as she took the box from him. She gently pulled at the red ribbon, took the top off the box and gasped.

Inside was a dazzling tiara that shimmered all over in white diamonds. It looked too dazzling to be real. Like there were live fairies living in the diamonds. It looked too delicate to pick up, so Faith just tipped the box slightly and showed it to Lex.

"Why would she give me a tiara?"

"It was hers; she wore it at her wedding. You grandmother wore it at hers and so forth and so on. It's an heirloom. She's bequeathing it you."

"To wear at my wedding?"

"Yes," said Lex with a pointed clearing of his throat. Clearly it was too soon to have that conversation. Before Faith could press the subject, she heard her phone ringing. She jumped up and sped to her bedroom where it was vibrating on her bedside table with Saoirse name flashing on it. Wanting to tell her all about the wedding, she picked it up and brought the phone to her ear.

"Soar, you are not going to believe the day I had," she said but then the voice she heard on the other end was not Saoirse's, it was Mitch's.

"Faith, you better come quick. It's Saoirse. She was hurt."

It took next to no time to make it Catrianna's home even though she had never been there before. Lex could only drop her off. He could not be seen there. So, she knocked on the door as he dissolved into wisp behind her. Mitch answered the door on the second knock. His face white as a sheet. His shirt stained with blood. Faith felt bile rise up in her throat at the site of it and Mitch caught her before she fell.

"Don't worry, she's out of danger," said Mitch. "I am only bloody cause I carried her in. Come and see her. She's been asking for you."

He led Faith to the living room, and she held her breath exhaling only when she saw Saoirse laying face up on a black sofa with all the members of the Affinity around her, Catrianna, Ambrosia and Daia. Faith shot the three of them a nasty look before she knelt down by

Saoirse's head. She was bandaged up all over from her arms to her legs. It was no wonder Mitch was covered in her blood.

"What on earth happened to you Soar?"

"Recruiting mission gone bad," mumbled Saoirse in a pained voice.

"GARGOYLE was recruiting again?"

"No, we were," said Ambrosia, sniffing. Her eyes puffy and red.

"GARGOYLE attacked us recruiting in Dorcela," said Catrianna. "Ironic huh? We've been doing it to them for so long, seemed only a matter of time."

"Or vengeance," said Daia in her misty voice then her white eyes found Faith. "We were attacked by Flammare and her troops and they went right for her. We had to fight them off her."

"Flammare did this to her!"

"Yep, your dear old sister attacked your best friend after all that time you spent with those demons, they obviously still don't trust you," Catrianna spat and a fire burned inside Faith and she made to lunge for her but she was halted by Daia holding up a hand and creating a magical forcefield between her and Catrianna. "Now is not the time for that."

"Faith, please don't fight," said Saoirse trying to sit up but Faith knelt back down and gently forced her back into a laying position.

"She was attacked by your sister, aren't you going to do anything about it?"

Faith did not know how to respond. After what she had Lex tell Nemfora, how could Flammare attack Saoirse and why? If it were revenge surely she would attack Catrianna. Or was Catrianna right and her sister was gunning for her best friend but to what end? None of it made sense. She had to get to the bottom of this and she knew she would not get answers from the Affinity, at least not the ones she wanted.

"Saoirse will heal right?" Faith asked Daia. "You can heal her?"

"It will take some time," said Daia, eyes turned down. "It will require some supplies from Resora but yes, she will make a full recovery in a day or two."

"Then I will leave you to it," said Faith standing up, her face hard.

"You're leaving?" raged Mitch. "But Saoirse needs you."

"I can't do anything for her here but worry," said Faith firmly. "I need to get to the bottom of what happened and why it happened."

"Crawling back to you little demon family?" Catrianna called to her retreating back but this Faith did not rise to her verbal attack.

"Keep me posted okay?" she said to Mitch, her hand briefly on his arm then she was out the door. She clutched the pendant around her neck and called for Lex. She did not want to feel it yet. Not until she was home. Not until she could be sure Catrianna was not on the other side of the door listening. It took 2 minutes for Lex to arrive. He did not say a word, just stared at the hard expression on her face and whisked her away.

As soon as they were back at the Andromeda, Faith screamed and fell to her knees, pounding the floor with her fist. Every pound she imagined the ground as Catrianna's face, and she pounded it even harder. She never really connected Saoirse being in the Affinity to her getting hurt or worse. Now the sight of her blood on Mitch, the sound of her pained voice, and her small body covered in bandages flashed over and over in her mind like a running nightmare.

Faith did not know how long Lex let her vent before he bent down and lifted her off the ground. Silent tears spilled down her face and she clung to him like a lifeboat.

"Cyphren told me what happened," said Lex in a low soothing tone. "Is Saoirse going to be alright?"

"Mmhmm," she mumbled. "I'm just in shock and angry Lex. I am so angry. How did this happen?"

Lex set her down on the bed but did not let go of her, settling half of her body on his lap and caressed her arms.

"Flammare decided to pay the Affinity back for their slight and not to mention the damage it did to her pride. She did not like being bested by an Affinity mage."

"Then why did go after Saoirse huh? Why not burn Catrianna or did she not know who injured her. They're both blonde after all."

"I don't know," said Lex. "She might have just wanted to make an example out of someone for the attack on her recruiting."

"Could be," said Faith but something about that just did not feel right. "From the way Catrianna described it, Flammare deliberately attacked her. She made it seem like Flammare did it to intentionally hurt me."

"And that's what confuses you isn't it, after what you revealed to them?"

Faith did not want to admit to that. Her sister used the information she provided her to attack her best friend.

"I thought we were making headway with GARGOYLE. I was a fool. I did this to her," Faith sobbed.

"What? No, it is not your fault," said Lex, wiping her tears away with a sweep of his thumb across her cheek. "Saoirse volunteered to be a member knowing the dangers. Knowing her mother died fighting Nemfora. I know Flammare, she would have wanted to even the score with or without your information."

Faith ignored his words and just picture Saoirse scared out of her wits with a girl who looked so much like her looking at her with a face full of malice. And then a thought came to Faith like a painful bolt of lightning.

"Lex, Flammare's never been off world right?"

"That's right thinks it will contaminate her," he scoffed.

"Was Cypren in the attack?"

"No, just Flammare and her personal troops."

"Then how did she what Saoirse looks like or even who she is to me?" Lex froze mid stroking her cheek.

"Did Cyphren tell her?"

"Cypren doesn't tell her anything," he replied, shaking his head. His sisterly affection only stretches to Catlinis. He is loyal to her. As far as he is concerned, Flammare is a threat to her future rule. He would not do something to help her."

"Then who told Flammare about Saoirse?"

"It would have to be someone at school who has access to Flammare," said Lex with a crinkled brow. "A mage like us."

"So that leaves Aubrey, Caprice and..." Faith's voice trailed off.

"And your half siblings, Rain and Storm."

Faith winced when he said their names, like each of them was a tiny needle in her ribs. Rain and her never got on but he did not seem interested in her enough to learn about her friends but Storm on the other hand wanted to spend time with her, get to know her. He could have easily watched her talking to Saoirse outside one day. Faith clutched her heart like the needle moved there with piercing prison. Rain betraying her was nothing. But she felt so close to Storm and the affectionate way he called her 'sis.' There was a warmth to his words when he said it. It felt real. Like a true bond was forming. Now it was Faith's turn to shake her head.

"It can't be Storm I just know it," said Faith, her voice rising at the end and Lex's eyebrow went up and she could feel his skepticism. "I can't explain how I know, I just do okay. It has to be one of the others."

"If that's what you believe, then I'll believe it to," said Lex firmly and Faith beamed up at him.

"But it makes me more worried for Saoirse and Dev and everyone else at school. And with the musical coming up."

"Yes, you're right to be worried if one of them is helping Flammare we need to protect the innocents," said Lex, his jaw clenched. He fell silent for a moment, then she saw light flicker in his eyes. "I will contact the Brotherhood and have some troops stationed at the school in disguise."

"You could do that?"

"Of course, my father would agree I am certain of it," he said with a reassuring smile. "I'll let him know so we can make the arrangements and choose the most inconspicuous mages for the job."

"You won't be long right?" she asked, the words leaving her lips before she could stop herself and she bit her lower lip. He pulled her face up until she was inches away from his own.

"I'll be back before you know it," he said with a swift kiss on her lips. "Love you."

"Love you too," she echoed, and her mouth spread into a wide smile. "Wow, that felt so natural." Grinning, Lex bent low and kissed her again, this time pressing his lips firmly to hers and twisting strands of her hair between his fingers. Then breathless and pink lipped, he caressed her face and disappeared from her side.

20

Requiem

"What hurt me was how unexpected it was. It hurt me to be so vulnerable and it hurt it my pride." – Faith

FAITH WAS JITTERY ALL morning on opening day of the musical. She did not leave Saoirse's side all day, grateful for the excuse of Saoirse's being second chair. No one could question her sticking to the water witch like glue. Like Daia said, she did make a full recovery, but Faith still opened doors for her, brought her all her meals and took her home every after school.

In spite of her reassurances that Storm was not the spy. Faith did not spend much time with the demon gang at school the days leading up to the musical. Pride had to provide many excuses for her absence and pout all through lunch without her at his side feeding him pudding.

Morning dress rehearsal was given priority over lessons so that provided another iron clad excuse. The orchestra ate lunch with the cast and crew in the dressing room above the auditorium.

Saoirse only ate grapes as she always did before shows or horse-riding competitions while Faith gave her a head massage. Today, her Dutch braids had red ribbons in them to match the red dresses all the girls had to wear. The boys had red ties and handkerchiefs in their suit jackets. Saoirse insisted on tying Faith's ponytail with a big red ribbon.

"Now we match," she said with a fluff of the ribbon to make it more rounded.

"I feel like that red dog from that book," Faith muttered looking at her reflection in the lighted mirror in the dressing room.

"You look adorable," Saoirse swore. "And hey, it matches your bracelet," She added, gesturing to the flames on her wrist. Faith looked down at the bracelet and a small corner smile escaped her lips and her mind went to the conversation she had with Lex that morning when he put the bracelet on her wrist.

"You sure they won't suspect troops to be at the musical?" Faith asked, a crease forming in her brow.

"GARGOYLE' target is the Prince on Dragonshire," said Lex as he fastened the bracelet clasp. "They won't suspect any security here."

"And the Brotherhood knows where they will attack and when?"

"They know."

"And Hope got away from Dragonshire safely?"

"Lord Malcom saw to it personally," Lex assured her. "She's in the safest place in Dorcela."

"Where's that?"

"Potential school."

"Potential school?" Faith repeated lifting an eyebrow. "What's so safe about a school."

"The location is completely secure," said Lex grinning and Faith's eyes narrowed. "It's secure because the location is completely impregnable by force. Only potentials can enter the school."

"For real? Who runs the school?"

"Past potentials."

"Ahhh."

"So, you see, she is perfectly safe. The Affinity has no involvement in the operation, so you don't have to worry about Saoirse. All you need to worry about is not messing up tonight."

"Gee thanks."

Back in the present, Faith was still a bundle of nerves; Shaking and wringing her hands. If it were not for the red lipstick, she would be biting her lips too.

"Jesus, I have never seen you this nervous before a show hun," Saoirse remarked, enclosing Faith in a one arm hug.

"We're on in one hour!" called the director from the other side of the door and girls shuttled around the dressing room making last minute touches to their make up while others practiced their music.

"Have you seen my left shoe?"

"Where's my reed?"

"I smudged my mascara."

"Come here, I have waterproof remover."

"Well at least you're in good company when it comes to nerves," Saoirse commented. "You sure you're okay, you seem...I don't know."

"I'll be fine," said Faith taking several deep breaths. "Just opening day jitters. Next show I'll be as fit as a fiddle."

"Okay, come, let's go over your solo, I'll lead you in."

Faith picked up her violin from the case beside her and brought it up to her neck, then with the bow in place and her eyes closed, she listening to Saoirse play her lead in and then her fingers did the rest. Playing had the exact desired effect Saoirse was looking for. The piece was soothing and beautiful and made Faith feel at ease. She was ready for the show and for GARGOYLE and whatever they each had in store for her.

Opening day of the musical rendition of Tristan and Isolde was sold out for weeks so Faith was not surprised to see every seat in the house filled when she and the rest of the orchestra took their seats. Sitting in the orchestra box felt safer than anywhere else in the auditorium. "I got this," she whispered then the conductor took his position, bowed and the show began with the opening of the curtains. Faith was so immersed in the music that she barely concentrated on what was going on stage. It was only when they were not playing that

Faith could see Devonte on stage. It was odd seeing him portray the role of the main antagonist, but he was such a good actor. She had to admit, Caprice did well as Isolde, but she was not nearly as pretty as she felt the role needed. After Act 1 ended without a hitch, Faith felt much of her anxiety leave her.

"Two more acts to go," said Faith and She looked up from the music for a moment to see Devonte wielding a sword. Then a cry sounded that was not in the script and Devonte fell to ground in a crumpled heap. Faith shot up out of her hair and saw a streak of red substance leave his body and travel in a in an upward trajectory. She followed its progression to a balcony box high above the stage, reserved for light fixtures and that is a when a tall willowy figure darted out of the box and out of sight. Faith made to leap into action and find the attacker but her she heard her name shouted.

"Faith come quickly. He's hurt!"

"Curtains, close the curtains at once and call an ambulance!"

Faith felt the color drain from her face. For days she was so worried about Saoirse that she never left his side. It never occurred to her that they would target Devonte. She stood perfectly still as the curtains closed on Devonte's unmoving body, but they stopped short with only a few inches left. She whipped around and saw everyone in the room not moving, gasping, or even blinking. Saoirse sobbed at her side but no one else made a sound and that is when a blinding light emitted from somewhere above them. Faith shut her eyes immediately, a fireball already forming in her hand, ready to attack but then when she blinked her eyes open, the figure of Daia appeared on the stage in front of her and then she knew.

"You stopped time," she said, fighting her way through the orchestra box and dragging the still sobbing Saoirse behind her. Ambrosia and Catrianna joined them from behind the curtain, Devonte floating in midair behind them. Forgetting Daia, Faith jumped on stage and tried to see where he had been hit but there was no puncture wound. No sign of blood or anything.

"What's going on?" she cried in Daia's direction.

"It appears he's been poisoned by a red dagger," said Ambrosia. "It's magical and leaves no traces except this." Ambrosia moved Devonte's collar and upon his mahogany skin was an imprint of a minuscule red dagger, like a tattoo except it glowed with sinister crimson hue.

"Flammare," Faith growled, bawling her fist.

"We're not so sure," came a voice Faith did recognize and she turned to see a squad of men dressed in black come down the tiered stairs in the middle of the auditorium and wielding weapons she could not name. But she knew they were Brotherhood troops from Lex's description of them. "Our intelligence says Flammare Bartuas has not left the realm, but the traces left behind the box used to attack the innocent were definitely female."

"Female?" Faith repeated. 'That rules out Rain and Storm.' Then she heard movement behind her turned back to the curtain. Everyone in the auditorium should still be frozen except their allies. Unless someone else was back there. Faith bounded behind the curtains and grabbed someone by their clothing. She dragged them back out on the stage. The girl struggled and kicked out by froze at the sight of the fire ball in Faith's other hand.

"Caprice Leah Landis, I should have shown," sneered Faith, the ball growing larger in her hand and Caprice's eyes widened with fear. "I think I'll kill you now."

"Wait!"

"I didn't do it, it wasn't me? I was on stage, how could have?" Caprice simpered.

"But you were feeding information to Flammare?" Faith accused her and she blanched.

"She forced me okay. I still have family in Dorcela you know."

"Well if you didn't attack her and Flammare isn't here, who did it?"

"Someone who hates you," Caprice spat. "Who's always hated and has been waiting for an opportunity to get her revenge on the Affinity and wanted to help Lady Flammare badly." Faith's mind flashed back to the tall figure she saw escape the box. She did it with a feline grace. She knew Devonte and Saoirse and certainly hated her enough to team up with Flammare.

"It was Rin wasn't it. Rin Kuwatani, the fallen?"

Caprice nodded, still whimpering in her grasp.

"She's back?" Saoirse breathed.

"We'll take care of her," said Catrianna, sparks flickering around her body. "She and I have unfinished business."

"You stay out of it?" Faith shouted but Daia stepped in between them.

"Let my girls deal with the fallen, they are better trained at this," she suggested then she looked to the Brotherhood squad. "You can escort the demon back to Dorcela."

They nodded and Faith dragged Caprice over to them where they magicked cuffs on to her wrist and disappeared with her.

"You can come out now nephew," Daia said out loud and Faith looked around wildly and Lex appeared behind her where she fell into his arms.

"Oh Lex."

"It's going to be okay Faith, you can heal him right Aunt Daia?"

Faith waited with bated breath as Daia approached the still floating and unconscious Devonte. Her hands glided over his body with her eyes closed, she mumbled something in a language Faith was unfamiliar with and then she winced and back away from him body.

"What's wrong, you can't heal him?" Faith cried.

"I can stabilize him and make sure the poison does not spread but we need Rin to reverse the effects."

"We will find her," said Saoirse, her face free of tears and full of determination. "I won't let her slip away this time."

"I trust you," said Faith giving her a swift hug then she and other Affinity members sped out the side door leaving her alone with Daia and Lex.

"What about this mess?" he asked, glancing around the frozen figures in the auditorium.

"It will take a lot of magic," she said slowly in her most mystical voice. "But I can make this night disappear from their memories. Opening night will have gone on successfully."

"Thank you Daia."

Faith peered at the unmoving form of Mitch nearly out of his seat in the front row and Faith found her resolve. She could not let this continue. She needed to confront Flammare and in person so no one else she cared for would be in danger of her again.

She looked up at Lex, jaw set and told him exactly what she wanted to do.

"Lex take me to Nemfora's castle," she demanded. "I want to have it out with Flammare."

"Are you nuts, you realize what you're asking me?"

"My nephew is right," Daia interrupted and Faith grumbled. "Flammare is more powerful than you. She is also a demimage with powers you know not."

"I don't care, this must end and thanks to the today's op Nemfora and most of GARGOYLE won't be in the castle right now."

"Even if it ends in your death?" said Lex darkly.

"Somehow I don't think it will come to that."

"You don't know her."

"She is still my blood," Faith argued. "It's that I need to appeal to. And I think I can, but I need to do this in person to get to the root of problem."

"You don't think it will come to blows? She'll be expecting an attack."

"If she wants a fight, I will give her one."

"Faith..."

"You're doubting me?"

"No, I just..."

"Look at me. Any part of me hesitating or scared?"

Lex's eyes traveled up and down her form and rested on her eyes that were looking right back at him unblinking.

"I have to do this Lex."

"I'll take you to her under one condition," he said staring at her with his somber eyes. "You talk to Damiel first."

Faith did not expect that. Seeing Damiel before Flammare almost weakened her resolve and she had the sinking suspicion that he was hoping her father would talk her out of confronting Flammare, but she would not budge, and she knew he would not either. So, if Flammare did destroy her, then she would not die not knowing her father.

"Deal, take me to him."

21

Father

"All I ever wanted was to be with the people I loved but having them all near would ignite Armageddon." – Anonymous

When Faith opened her eyes, she did not waste time taking in the sights of Nemfora's kingdom. That is not what she was there for. Her dreary castle held her no fascination for her. Lex dropped her off right at Damiel's door and he was certain he was inside.

"Do what you have to do, I will keep anyone from returning too early," he said giving her a lingering hug and a kiss. "Summon when you need me."

"I will."

"I love you."

"I love you too."

And with that, he was gone, leaving Faith standing in front of his door.

"I can do this," she whispered then balled her fist and knocked on the door.

"Enter."

The wooden door opened with a creak and she walked in taking in the scent of stale ale and firewood burning. Sitting in front of the fire with a white cat on his lap. The cat leapt from his knees when it caught sight of Faith and the man sitting in the chair stood up and stared at her. Eyes hard and barely registering her then they narrowed, and his face was unreadable. His face which should have been unfamiliar to her was not. His face which should have repulsed her, did not. Somewhere inside her she felt a longing she could not explain. Like someone magnetic force was pulling her towards Damiel until she was standing right in front of him.

"Faith?"

"Dad?"

Strong arms enclosed around her and Faith wanted to recoil but she did not. It took all of her resolve not to return the hug but keep her arms firmly at her side. He released her quickly then sat back down. The white cat rested on the mantlepiece eyeing her suspiciously like it was afraid she would hurt Damiel.

"Why are you here? Did anyone see you come in?"

"I was careful," she said taking the seat opposite in front of hearth and the cat leapt back on to his lap.

"Why have you come? Do you know what's happening today?"

"That's why I could come," she said.

"Smart, like your mother."

Upon hearing that faith felt some of her rage and hatred for him return.

"Like my mother, like the mother your fo...," she started but Faith found that she could not get the words out.

"I loved your mother," Damiel sneered.

"Bull!"

"You don't know that whole story. Our story."

"What is there to tell. I already heard the whole story how you seduced her."

"Let me guess, you heard this so-called full story from Maurice or an old friend of your mother's," said Damiel and Faith fell silent but then she countered him.

"And let me guess, you say there's more to it than what they told me," she said, eyes piercing into his. Eyes shaped so much like her own. The same length, the same long eyelashes. Only the irises were different.

"Did anyone tell you that we both grew up in Empyrion or that we went to the same school?" he asked, and Faith's jaw dropped.

"What? No, you are lying! You didn't! You couldn't have! It was a girl's school."

"The boy's school was on the other side of the campus. What reason would I have to lie now Faith?" he argued. "You could leave now and check the school records or even the town's records and find my name."

"If you knew her why..?"

"Why did turn out the way it did? Bad luck. Bad timing and a destiny she couldn't escape."

"Potential school," Faith guessed, and he nodded, stroking the cat's back with his large hand. It purred loudly in response.

"I was some moon cycles older than your mother, but we lived near each other and that's how we got acquainted. She liked the tricks I could do with fire and I was drawn to her light. The gift of being a potential but we did not know then. When she entered the school after me, it became clearer and clearer that our friendship would soon end. Her talents were legendary. The things she could do, no other potential her age could. The day she was taken away, she gave me Yulani."

He gestured to cat on his lap and Faith looked from the cat to him and suddenly she felt for him. Her mother was leaving him, and she gave him something to remember her by.

"She was a newborn then, but I nursed her and raised her and kept her with me always thinking one day I could return it to her but then my own destiny caught up with me."

"What destiny?"

"I was...promised to Nemfora. Betrothed at birth."

"You had an arranged marriage?" she said incredulously. "But what about Kemrick?"

"Kemrick was her exception. Her choice. Once he was dead, she was bound to marry me once more.

"A marriage I never thought would happen," he said, and Faith could hear the anguish in his voice. "My father agreed that if I met and proposed to someone else before Nemfora came of age, I would not have to marry her. But your mother was unreachable."

"Non potentials couldn't travel to the school," said Faith and he nodded.

"So, I married Nemfora even though my parents knew what kind of person she'd become. They like many others had anti Higher Order sentiments and thought I made the better choice. My choice was unfavorable. I tried to forget your mother. But then she showed up here undercover as a demimage. I could not believe my eyes when I saw her in disguise, but her light was the same. I knew it was her. I promised to keep her secret from Nemfora, and I kept my word."

"I was told you threatened her and Maurice?" Faith countered remembering Lex's words.

"I would never have revealed your mother to Nemfora, not ever. What she told her friend was her business and to keep him from finding out our connection," he said. "I thought I had forgotten my love for her, that I had moved on, but those feelings never went away. On the night of Flammare's birth I presented Chryselda with Yulani and told her I needed to forget her for the sake of my children and their future. I wanted to leave her in the past but when I put Yulani in her arms and walked away from her she called out for me in my old nickname, 'Dami' and then I was lost. She was in my arms and we were declaring our love for each other once again."

"How could I believe any of this?" said Faith. She knew Lex had not lied to her so if Damiel's story was true, than her mother lied to him.

"You must have heard stories about your mother, about her strength about her powers," he said, and Faith nodded curtly still not believing him. "Do you really think I could have done anything to her without her putting up a fight? Heck your mother could have chopped my head clean off with her energy alone."

"Why would she lie?"

"To protect everyone involved, that included her friend who she did not want wrapped up in her troubles. She said he suffered enough. That a destiny was waiting for him that she could not interfere with. Even as she lay dying in my arms after you were born. One of her last words to me were 'If it is my destiny to die for my child then I will do it without hesitation. My death is tied to her destiny. I am sorry and forgive me for not sparing you this.'"

At this, Faith heard a voice in her mind. A voice she knew. A voice she heard before. "Faith, my Faith. I leave it to you. You Faith are my hope for a future free of Nemfora," said the voice and tears spilled down her face. Damiel looked at her aghast, the cat leapt from his lap and on to hers and licked her face.

"Yulani?" Faith whispered and it ceased licking and stared at her. She reached out and stroked its head hearing its gentle purr. Then she looked over at Damiel.

"I don't what to believe," she said finally.

"It's a lot to take in," he said, his eyes on the fireplace. "But your mother also said this. When you come into your full powers, you will be able to know what she knows."

"You mean, see the future like her?" she asked, and he shrugged. "You mother was very cryptic."

"You don't say."

"Still you haven't told me why you're here."

"Oh!" she said loudly, startling Yulani who jumped back on to the mantlepiece. "Sorry, but I need to see Flammare," she added, and she rushed into a hurried explanation careful to leave out any mention of Lex. From his story he had no idea who Lex was.

"So, you're here to confront my daughter?"

"That's right."

"Are you trained in combat?"

"Yes."

"Then I won't stop you."

"You won't!" she kind of thought he would especially after the story he told her.

"This is between the two of you. You need to solve this between yourselves," he said plainly as Yulani returned to his lap and his gaze returned to the fire. "I'll just give you one bit of advice. We are blood you and I that's why we feel a pull towards each other."

"You saying I'll feel it with her too like with Storm?"

"Yes, your Bartuai blood burns like fire within you because Flame ignites Flame but remember this. Flame cannot undo Flame. Never forget that. You'll find her in the throne room or just follow the pull."

22

Flame

"I don't know what a sister really is because I never really experienced having one." – Faith

FAITH LEFT DAMIEL'S room and shut her eyes. The magnetic pull she felt to Damiel was on her right but she felt something else pulling her from somewhere below, so she concentrated hard on it while thinking 'Take me there' in her mind and that's when she felt her feet leave the ground and her whole body was engulfed in soft flames before her surroundings disappeared. Her feet touched solid ground what felt like seconds later and the flames were gone. 'That's the first time I flame traveled on my own. And because I was thinking about Flammare which means she's in here with me.'

Faith opened her eyes and found herself facing a set of thrones and there was a girl standing in front of easily largest and most elaborate one. She had about a foot of jet-black hair in a high ponytail and an outfit of some black material that hugged her defined form. Faith could tell from the distance between them that she was muscular. Something in the still air told her that Flammare would not go down easily. Her father's warnings were enough to make her cautious but not enough to stop her.

"I knew you'd come little sister," came the husky voice of Flammare and she whipped around to face her, and Faith clapped her hands to her mouth. It was then that she understood what the others meant. They did resemble each other. The texture and color of their hair was different, and their skin tone differed, but their bone structure was the same. The same nose, the same eyes, jawline, and high cheek bones.

"How?"

"Flame blood Faith," she said so nonchalantly that she looked bored. "Can't escape it. The Bartuai are special. The Flame that runs through me runs through you but it's that same Flame that makes me hate you with every fiber of my being."

"Why, what did I do to you but be born?" Faith shouted.

"That's just it Faith. You exist. There should be one Princess of the Flame and that's me."

"Princess of the what? I don't care about anything like that. I'm not from here I don't care about titles. I care about you hurting my friends."

"Oh that," said Flammare and a wicked grin spread across her face. "That was to get you here. See I know you'd come."

"And what exactly do you want from me?"

"Your flame spent!" she cried with a lunge, but Faith leapt aside just in time. Her feline instincts kicked in at just the right moment. Faith threw balls of flame in her direction, but she dodged each of them with effortless agility, umping and flipping out of the way like a star gymnast.

"That the best you could do little sister," she taunted. "I am Flammare Bartuas, Flame Mare of the Bartuai. I was raised to be warrior. You were raised to play silly songs on a violin."

"Okay, you're fast, just how fast are you?" Faith challenged and she spread her arms wide as small flames appeared on her back and tied themselves together like spiderwebs to make a set of glowing red wings. The malice on Flammare's face was palpable.

Now she had to work extra hard to dodge her flames. She threw them with both hands this time, the blast growing larger and larger until at last she was blasted by a direct hit and fell to the ground. Still in the air, Faith looked down to see if she was able to get back up but then she felt something wrap itself around her foot and tug her down. A thin red rope from Flammare's hand tied itself to her. Faith fell to the ground with a thud, then she rolled over and was airborne again but there was a noticeable burnt flesh in shape of Flammare's whip across her skin.

Now it was Faith's turn to dodge as Flammare tried to catch her with her whip again while simultaneity throwing tiny balls of flame herself and she was growing more tired by the second. She had to find a way to incapacitate her.

There was one move she learned from practicing with Storm, but it was dangerous. It would work but it would hurt Faith too. Faith flew as high as the ceiling would allow her and gathered up as much energy in her right hand as possible while her wings emitted enough power to steady her. Flammare was not going to give her time to charge the attack as she sent jets of flame her way. But Faith's wings expanded large enough to block them by wrapping around her body like a cocoon and giving her plenty of time to charge. Just when she thought she'd built up enough energy, Faith opened her wings and sent it hurtling towards Flammare, too large to dodge but her sister wasn't complacent, Faith saw the largest blast of flame heading her way as well and she screamed and folded her wings to take the hit but she wasn't fast enough and the blast hit hard enough to knock her out of the sky. The ground was coming at her too fast and she braced herself to hit it but then she felt herself slowing down and the impact did not hurt as much as she thought it should.

She peered across the throne room and found Flammare laying on ground in front of her. Not terribly hurt but injured enough not to take flight again, Faith limped over to her ready to give the final blow but then she was blown back by a sudden gust of wind just as Flammare was straining to get up. Her once neat black clothes were scorched leaving gaping holes in the fabric. Faith looked around to see where the blast had come from to see Lex as Pride standing between them holding up his hands.

"Leafander stay out of this!" Flammare called.

"That's enough!" came a voice from behind Faith and she whipped around to see her father standing there with Yulani running around his feet.

"Father!"

"I said enough," he repeated this time with much more force and a burning in his eyes that even frightened Faith. "You've both proven how talented you are in the ways of flame. Let this be the end of it. More to that you'll never be able to fatly wound each other."

"What do you mean father?" Flammare growled.

But Faith understood. "It's what you said to me, Flame cannot undo Flame."

"What, the old Bartuai saying?"

"It's not just a saying Mare its true," said Damiel. "The two of you could fight until you're both mentally and physically exhausted but you'll never fatally wound each other with the flame. Your blood won't allow you to."

"It's bull."

"It's magic," Pride interrupted. "You noticed both of your wounds are just on your flesh. The last blast from Faith should have torn you to pieces but you absorbed some of the attack and it protected you."

"You knew this would happen?" Faith asked and Pride just nodded.

"Let this be the end Mare," said Damiel but she just glared at him. "Mare!"

"It's done dad. I won't...interfere with your pathetic Off World life if you'd stop trying to encroach on mine."

"What have I done?"

"Storm, my father, my mother, I feel like I'm being replaced by a newer model," Flammare cried out but it was Damiel she was speaking to not Faith and that is when she understood. The root of Flammare's hatred for Faith was fear of losing those closest to her. It was a feeling she could relate to.

"Mare, you are my daughter, nothing will change that. You have my name and my love. Faith doesn't want a life here, am I right."

Faith just nodded.

"Storm will always be your brother, but you can't stop the bond they have formed. It's in their blood. Would you want hurt him?"

"Of course not!"

"Then stop this," he pleaded. "Accept that Faith is a part of this family but it does not mean she needs to be a part of your life. Your life is here. Her life is there."

"What about mom?"

"I will speak to her on this matter but having Faith in GARGOYLE does not replace you. It never will you understand me."

"Yes, dad."

"Now go and have the healers see to your burns before your mother sees you."

Flammare sent Faith a cold stare then she was gone in a burst of flame.

"Thank you your Grace," said Pride kneeling before Damiel and Faith made her way over to them. "I don't think I could have stopped them on my own."

"I did what I did to protect my children. Both of them."

"Dad, what happens now?"

"You go back to the human world with Pride and try to harness your other abilities. The ones passed to you by your mother," said Damiel and Faith looked up at him just as he pressed something into her palm. She opened it and found a pendant in the shape of a star with white diamonds like the ones in her tiara from her aunt Lucia. Pride craned his neck to see what was in her hand then his eyes shot to Damiel.

"That's the star pendant!"

"What's a star pendant?"

"It's proof of lineage," said Pride turning to face her, his eyes very wide. "Proof of potential lineage."

"Potential! But I'm not...I thought Hope was."

"You are," said Damiel, putting a hand on her shoulder and she felt warmth radiating from his hand like he had given her a hug. "Your mother gave me this to give to you, not Hope. She is a potential, but you are too. The mere fact that you could you see visions is proof you're a potential."

"It is?" she said, and she looked at Pride who nodded.

"But lineage itself is not enough to prove you're the next star. You can already see and talk to the dead right? Hear your mother's voice sometimes? I recognized the symptoms when you were in my study."

"The dead?" Pride repeated, rounding on Faith who shrunk under his gaze. "Since when?"

"Since always."

"And you didn't tell me?"

"I was scared, I didn't understand what I was seeing."

"It's to prepare you," said Damiel, gripping her shoulder tightly but not painfully. "Prepare you for your final test to prove you are the Star of Dorcela. The final test requires you to summon your Star ancestors. Faith, you have to learn to summon your mother from the heavens to this realm."

"You're out of your mind I can't do that!"

"Pride explain it to her," said Damiel and he looked around as they all heard noises from somewhere else in the castle. "You must go now, back Off World. Pride tell her what she needs to know. Go now."

"Come on," said Pride taking her hand and holding her close.

"Will I ever see you again dad?"

He gave her a weak smile just as Yulani leapt into his arms.

"You will, I promise."

And with those last words, he and the castle were gone, and Faith found herself in a white room she did not recognize.

"Where did you take us?"

"The hospital to check on.."

"Dev! Where is he?" she'd completely forgotten about him but as she looked around the room she realized they were alone in an empty hospital room.

"I had to teleport us to an empty room just in case there were mortals in Devonte's room," Lex explained as he opened the door. "He's across the hall."

Faith sped out of the room and spun around wildly until she heard familiar voices in the room just to the right of the one they arrived in. The door was opened, and it sounded like a lot of people were talking. She darted in the room and found Devonte sitting up in a white bed with Mitch, Saoirse, Ambrosia and Catrianna standing around his bed.

"Faith, you came back!" said Saoirse.

"Hey cuz," said Devonte brightly.

"How is he?" Faith demanded.

"He's going to be okay," said Ambrosia. "We found Rin. Daia is holding her captive, but there will be some lasting effects to healing Devonte."

"What do you mean?" she asked and pushed her out of the way to examine Devonte herself. But he looked perfectly fine.

"She had to unseal his abilities to heal him cause the poison had spread too much," said Catrianna who was standing next to Mitch with his arm around her waist, but Faith found that it no longer bothered her.

"Wait a minute. You mean Devonte is a mage again?" said Faith.

"Yep, I'm a freak just like you cuz," said Devonte grinning and Saoirse smacked him on the arm.

"But you can seal them again, can't you or Daia?" said faith looking from Ambrosia to Catrianna but they both shook their heads.

"Once unsealed, its magically irreversible," Ambrosia explained. "He is back to being a mage. Which means..."

"Which means he has to be trained," Catrianna finished.

"Leave that to me," said Lex from the doorway.

"You're undercover," said Catrianna icily and Faith felt some of her hatred for her coming back. "Don't want him taught to be a demon."

"I don't mean me specifically," he said ignoring Catrianna's insult. "I mean I know people who can come here to train him. He is dragon kind after all. He should be trained by a dragon kind teacher."

"Dragon kind?" Faith mouthed

"I'll explain later."

"Well you are right about that, he is technically a Spiritwolfe," said Ambrosia thoughtfully.

"Do I have a say in this?" Devonte asked and nearly everyone in the room said "No."

23

Birth right

"I know what I am expected to do but I don't how to do it." – Faith

T he last days of school were a blur. Devonte took a leave of absence and was whisked off to Dragonshire to train with Malcom until the start of the next term. Nemfora's plan to kidnap the Prince had failed thanks to the Brotherhood so Dragonshire was once again secure. Devonte's understudy had to do the remainder of the shows for him. Faith felt a kind of emptiness with him gone but she had something new in her life to occupy her time, learning how to summon.

Lex took her to their usual training spot on the old campus but this time instead of learning combat, she was meditating and reading a lot of old books on the philosophy behind summoning. Since the act of summoning released a lot of energy, it was unsafe to practice it in her apartment.

"I don't get how learning how to summon is so important," said Faith, nearly tossing the book she was holding in frustration as she failed again to light the summoning circle.

"Your father did not have time to explain it to you," said Lex and he took Faith's hand in his own and held it against his chest.

"Summoning the dead is an integral duty a Star must perform."

"Why, it's so morbid."

"Because Star's are assisted and guided in their duties by their ancestral Stars," Lex tried to explain. Faith cocked her head to the side and blinked several times and then she finally got it.

"Wait...you mean if it turns out I am the true next Star of Dorcela, my mother's spirit will guide me?"

"Yes," said Lex, his eyes twinkling. "You'll be able to talk to her every day and she'll teach you everything you need to know."

"I'll have mom back," Faith whispered unable to contain her happiness. To able to speak with her mother even in spirit form was more than could have dreamed of.

"But there's more Faith," said Lex, his tone serious and she gestured for him to continue.

"If you perfect this ability and summon Chryselda back to this plane of existence, you will not only be recognised as the next true Star of Dorcela, you will have the power to destroy Nemfora and all of GARGOYLE for good."

Epilogue

The duties of the Star of Dorcela are so many. It's like being a Queen with no subjects. The public appearances, the hand holding, the healing rites, the ceremonies, and the blessings are just my official duties. There are duties in the afterlife. Once a Star, always a Star. It is a lifelong position that does not end when your life does. AC once asked me, would I accept this position if I knew just how much I would be asked to do? I thought a lot about it and about the people I've met, healed, blessed or counseled. I know that I have touched their lives. Could someone else have done my job the way I did it? Would someone else care for the people the way I do? Those questions and more flooded my mind the moment he asked me, and I knew my answer would be yes. My duties may be many, may be taxing, may keep me in a cage but I was born a Star I can't live any other way. - Chryselda Star of Empyrion

Preview the next book

"I never thought I'd be back here," Faith muttered under her breath, struggling to keep her face neutral. Lex stood beside her as Pride in full regalia looking like the Prince he pretended to be. Lex nudged her with his mind, and she silenced herself. They were in a completely different room from the first time they visited this castle, so Faith took her time in admiring the décor. It was nothing like Lex's castle in Empyrion with its towering pillars, floating lights, and open-air rooms.

Where Lex's castle was full of gold and white, this castle was full of color. The draperies, the tablecloths, the carpet even the uniforms the guards wore. And there always food on every available surface. Faith imagined the people of this kingdom to be very well fed indeed.

Their throne room remind Faith more of the throne room in Nemfora's domain with its high ceilings and stone walls. Faith had a shrewd idea the reason for the high ceiling and it was this reason that kept her glued to Lex's side in anticipation.

Unlike Nemfora's abode, this castle only had three thrones. At present they were empty and there was ample space in front of them and between them. Faith's heart raced when she looked at the wide empty space beside the smallest throne. 'That's where she'll be,' she thought. Then at once, there was a clatter above them, and Faith's eyes shot up to see the ceiling dissolving like the entrance gates did on their first visit.

This display of magic had something else more magnificent to capture Faith's attention. As she stared up, three figures descended from the ceiling on top to three bridled dragons with bejeweled heads and colorful saddles. Faith's fingers dug into Lex's arm who winced at her side as the dragons and their rides took their positions next to their thrones. Faith thought that would be their display of magical might and high standing, but they did not even dismount the dragons. Instead, the riders themselves dissolved into mist and appeared in their dazzling thrones moments later. The dragons remained where they were but they lowered to a sitting position and folded their wings at their master's side.

Faith had to stop herself from rolling her eyes but in her head she said, 'Puh lease. Was that even necessary?'

A guard standing to the far right of the grandest throne cleared his throat.

"Presenting, His Royal Highness Prince Vashaun, His Lordship the Duke of Dragonshire Malcom Spiritwolfe and the Honorable Duchess of Dragonshire, Hope Spiritwolfe."

Faith looked up at the haughty face of her half sister as she looked down at her with narrowed eyes and pursed lips. A face that once declared how happy she was to meet her now looked at with such distain that Faith felt that she might bore into ground in embarrassment. But Faith was not going give her the satisfaction. She threw back her gorgeous head of luminous curls and smiled back at her broadly with a slight smirk in the corner of her mouth, careful to hold Lex's hand tightly as she did so.

Peak at my New Series
The Light of Darkness
The Orion Twins

"*I have always been seen as a strong person*
Everyone thinks I have the strength to withstand anything.
But they do not know that I only appear to be strong.
They do not see the weaker side of me that I keep hidden.
They see my outer shell but not my fragile insides.
I must be strong for the sake of my family.
But for how long can I keep up this façade,
Before someone realizes that I am not as they think I am.
How long before my suit of armor has taken all the hits it can take,
And I am left there naked and weak?"

August 24th started out as an ordinary day for the Orion twins. They woke up, scared their caregiver Mrs. Horne, had breakfast, then sat next to each other in silence as the other children played. There they sat hand in hand in the playroom talking only to each other. None of the other children seem to acknowledge their existence. When they first arrived at the orphanage, this annoyed them but now it was commonplace. They were used to being ignored by the other kids and treated badly by the staff who did not want them there.

The Orion's Hunter and Liberty were the oldest children at the St. Helen's Orphanage in Canterbury England at nearly 15 years old. They had been back and forth from foster homes 7 times. The reasons varied; one family called them freaks and said they frightened the other children. Another said they drove her into insanity with their antics.

Around the age of 11 they were sent back after a mysterious fire in the house. The orphanage then thought of separating them.

By the end of the first day they spent apart, Liberty began crying about a splitting headache. Her foster parents thought she was lying until she passed out from the pain. She was sent to the hospital, but the doctors did not know how to help her.

Hunter's foster mother was notified, and he was rushed to see her. As soon as he entered her room, she woke up. After that incident they were not ever separated by the orphanage. Four years had passed since then incident and they weren't ever considered for foster care again. At the age 15, the twins thought that they would never find a home. However, on August 24th someone came to the orphanage who would change their lives forever.

"Ni-san?" said Liberty staring at the odd expression on her brother's face. "What is it?"

"I sense something; some powerful is coming this way."

"Or someone." Hunter finished. "We have to be on our guard."

"It could be them."

"You think they found us after all these years?" Hunter asked

"Who's to say they ever stopped looking for us?" said Liberty her eyes darting from left to right. 'Maybe we're finally on their radar."

" If you're right we need to get out of here and fast nee-chan."

At that moment both of their eyes darted to the doors as Mrs. Horne entered.

"There is someone here to see you," she said with a look of shock that matched their own shocked faces. Hunter grabbed Liberty's hand as they stood up and followed Mrs. Horne out of the room. They were both ready to attack whatever was waiting for them.

As they entered the conference room a woman stood up and turned around. She was strikingly beautiful, tall, and radiant with black hair that curled around her neck, dazzling green eyes and a kind face.

They stood speechless staring at her. "I'll leave you to talk," Mrs. Horne said as she backed out of the room and closed the door.

"Who are you?" Liberty asked.

'Evil sometimes comes with a kind face' she projected to Hunter.

"Something your mother taught you no less." Said the woman suddenly

"You can...?"

"Read your thoughts, yes. You should be more guarded."

Hunter stepped in front of Liberty ready to strike. "We'll ask again, who are you?"

"No one who would cause you any harm I assure you."

"How do we know we can trust you?"

"You don't." said the woman

There was silence and then Liberty spoke but this time she seemed more annoyed as she was losing her patience.

"I've had had enough. Either you tell who you are, or we start using force." The woman looked strangely impressed.

"Very well," she said "I am Aulia, your mother's sister, which makes me your aunt."

Hunter and Liberty looked at each other in amazement, then back to Aulia.

"Why are you here after all these years?" Liberty asked still not ready to trust the strange woman.

"Because it has taken me quite sometimes to find you even though the spell your mother cast has lifted."

"Wait okasan's spell has been lifted?" they said in unison, a look of horror written on their faces. Aulia looked away sadly.

"Before okasan left us here she said she cast a spell to keep people from finding us." Hunter started

"The spell can only be lifted two ways. First it she does it herself in which case she will come and get us herself. The second is if she is...killed," said Liberty as she leaned on Hunter for support.

"No she can't be," said Hunter angrily as he turned and embraced Liberty "She promised. She promised she'd be back for us. She promised us."

"I am sorry," said Aulia slowly as she handed Hunter an envelope. He released Liberty and took it. He opened it cautiously.

"It's from mom."

"Read it," said Liberty

"Dear Rin and Shinji

If you are reading this, then my spell has been lifted and my sister Aulia is with you. I am sorry your father and I can't be there to take you away from that place. Your father and I are working on a very important mission and we don't know when it will be safe to collect you. That is why I have sent Aulia. When the time comes, we will be reunited again. Right now, your safety is more important than anything. Until then,

Shinji looked after your sister.

Rin be strong.

Love you

Mom"

"It's definitely authentic; she addressed us by our real names," said Liberty

"Does this mean that they are still alive?" Hunter asked hopefully

"That I do not know. The last time I saw your parents was the day she gave me that letter and that was a year ago," said Aulia and Hunter looked crestfallen.

"That means nothing ni-san. They both could still be alive out there. Whatever mom and dad are doing out there they are doing it for us so we can live freely without constantly looking over our shoulders for the enemy." said Liberty confidently.

"So what happens now?" Hunter asked

"Now we leave this place. I'm taking you back home."

"Home?" they said in unison

"Yes your home."

Aulia filled out all the necessary paperwork as the twin sat in silence waiting. Finally, they were going to leave the orphanage for good. They were finally going to be told the truth about their parents and their birth right. What kind of future awaits the Orion twin? And who are the invisible threat that they have been avoiding all these years?

"Everything is ready," said Aulia and the Orion's left with her. They had very few things as the never received gifts from anyone. All they had with them were a few clothes and mementos given to them by their parents. They only had enough things to fill two duffle bags. Hunter and Liberty took one last glace at the small stone orphanage then they got in the taxi hoping to never to see that place again. A day later they exited the airport to arrive in Tokyo, Japan where the battle for their future begins.

CHAPTER ONE - CHANCE Meetings

"Alone
Even when surrounded by people I feel alone.
Even with him by my side I feel alone.
I have felt this way for a long time, but I hide it from him.
I He tires his best to comfort me
But what I need he can't give me.
I need someone else to take this pain away.
How much longer can I mask my pain from him?
How much longer will I live with this loneliness?
Am I dammed to always be alone because of what I am?"

HUNTER AND LIBERTY arrived at a very large home in an upscale area. Liberty recognized the house the moment she set eyes on it. It was a two-story white mansion with the kanji 'Tachibana' written on the gates. Beyond the gates were statues and small fountain surrounded by exotic flowers. Hunter was speechless as he walked up the familiar stairs to the front door.

"I kept it just as they did leave it. Your rooms as well," said Aulia "Even though no one in the family lived here; the servants continued to clean and kept the gardens tended to. We always knew that you two would come back."

The two of them walked slowly into the luxurious home. It was as if time was frozen in the house. Even though they had not entered it for many years, it looked exactly as it had when they left it. In the drawing room there was a family portrait of them. Their mother and father were sat on chairs with 4-year-old Hunter and Liberty standing on either side of them.

"Mom...dad," they whispered gently

"Let's have a look upstairs," said Liberty and Hunter nodded. The two of them walked slowly upstairs and turned right. Hunter's room was the first door on the right-hand side. He slowly turned the knob and opened the door. A wave of emotions over swept him as he took in the familiar surroundings. Not a single article was misplaced. Liberty had similar reaction to her room. Coupled with the joy of being back home was this feeling of intense emptiness as their parents were no were in sight. The two of them walked back downstairs hand in hand. Not a word was spoken between them as the both felt equally as miserable.

Aulia was waiting for them in the family room. "Are you ready?" she asked

"For what?" they asked

"The truth."

The two of them sat down on the sofa in front of her and then nodded. I guess I should start with from the beginning. A very long time ago there existed a religion called the Followers of Light. These people worshiped the Goddess of Light, Hikari. It is written that once day a great calamity would befall the world and a chosen vessel was used to harness the power of Hikari and save the world. The women from my family, your family had the power necessary to be possessed by Hikari. My mother was a vessel, but she was killed 10 years ago, so another vessel was chosen." Aulia looked to Liberty.

"Me?" she said and Aulia nodded

"But since you were only 7 at the time, any easy target for forces that might want to use you. It was then decided that you two be sent away. You each had your names changed and were sent off to England."

"Why couldn't we stay with you at first?" Hunter asked

"I was only a teen at the time."

"Don't we have relatives in England, I men our father is from there right?"

"Yes but the enemy would expect that."

"So the only choice our parent had was to abandon us in a foreign country?" Liberty asked

"They had no choice. They did it for your safety. Hunter you and you alone possess the powers need to protect your sister. You know this."

"Yes I've always known," said Hunter "Father told me I am meant to protect her he just never told me exactly why. I mean I know she is my sister, but he made it sound like it was birth right."

"It is." Each vessel is assigned someone is who has the powers needed to protect them from evil. Hikari may be a Goddess but in the body of the vessel she is vulnerable.

"Who are they, the enemy I mean?" Liberty asked and Aulia hesitated for a moment.

"They are a rival clan. A family who thought they had the right to be vessels for they worshipped Hikari as well. As powerful as their family maybe be, there hasn't been a vessel born into their family for many centuries. The family of vessel is treated as royalty. Their family was jealous. In retaliation they began killing vessels in the hopes that the next one would be born into their family. Their family still exists today but their goal is more sinister now. They have turned their back on Hikari for they feel she has turned her back on them. I am not clear on their goal, but it was worse than death for my mother allowed herself to be killed in order to avoid being used by them. This is why your parents are not here. They are working hard to stop that clan from trying to get to you."

Liberty felt strange. She did not realize she was so important. But she also felt angry that she was chosen against her will to be the saviour of the world. To have such a big responsibility weighing on her shoulder was overwhelming. Hunter felt proud. He lover his sister very much and he would die to protect her. She was the most important person in his life.

"So what happens now?" Liberty asked

"Now you go on about your lives as normal. Keep your powers to yourselves and don't draw any unnecessary attention to yourselves. They're still people out there that would harm you until we hear otherwise from your parents. Hunter sighed. Keeping a low profile would prove to be difficult for them. Each of them was born with unique powers.

Since she was very young, Liberty could read the thoughts of others and feel people's emotions. Her mother told her that it was a gift however Liberty always thought of it as a curse. Everyday other people thoughts invade her mind and when it got to be too much it would cause her immense pain. She could not shut her power off and on as she pleased but she had gained some control over it over the years. The only time her mind was free of other people's thoughts was when her brother was near her. She does not why bit she is grateful for it.

Hunter was born with telepathy, the mental ability to move objects. He could also move air molecules and other matter and turned into a solid mass creating a force field for anyone behind it. Most of the time he could keep his powers in check but whenever he lost his temper things would float around him also whenever Liberty was in danger, he would automatically put up a force filed without commanding his powers to do so.

Keeping their powers secret was enough of a problem but their unique appearance attracted a lot of attention. Hunter was quite tall for his age and muscular. His skin was pale as ivory. His silky black hair caressed his cheeks and it fell in front of his eyes. But his hair could not shield people from his sapphire blue eyes which gleamed like blue orbs behind his hair.

Liberty was equally just as tall with ivory colored skin. Her wavy black hair reached her lower back and was parted in the middle so that her silver eyes were in clear view. They were both strikingly attractive, but their pale skin and odd colored eyes made people stray way from them. Sometimes people would point and stare at them. None of the other kids at the orphanage would play or even approach them. They were all afraid of them even the adults.

"Normal huh?" said Liberty thinking about the reaction they got walking around the street and in airport. That night Hunter and Liberty spelt on their parent's bed. Their familiar sent lingered in the room. After a few days of getting used to the time change, Aulia had planned an interview with a local school.

"Seiryu Academy is a good school. Very prestigious," said Aulia on their way to the interview.

"It's no different if we went to a common school," Liberty started

"We'd still get treated the same way," said Hunter

"What do you mean?" Aulia asked

"We're just used to being treated like..."

'Freaks."

"You're not freaks you're special."

"Special is just a nice way of saying freak," said Liberty

"Don't," Hunter warned Aulia he noticed her about to argue. "You don't know what we've been through."

The rest of the ride continued in silence. As they waited in the office to see the Principal, they received odd looks from the staff. They only stopped looking when Liberty glared at them.

"I have to use the toilet," said Hunter"Do you want someone to take you?" Aulia asked

"No" said Hunter standing up. "I think I saw one on our way in here." Hunter nodded to Liberty then he left the office. He looked up and down the hall trying to remember where he saw the means room. He turned left and walked slowly down the hall. He heard footsteps then a person appeared to right of him. Hunter turned with a start. A pair of onyx eyes met his.

"Excuse me, are you allowed to be wondering the halls?" the boy asked as he brushed his silky black hair out of his eyes to get a better look at him. Hunter took a step back from him. The boy looked him up and down and Hunter thought he saw him smirk. "Well?"

"I'm here for an interview. I just need to use the toilet," said Hunter nervously. He tried to avoid the boy's onyx eyes but he kept staring at him as if hypnotized. This boy was only little taller than him with dark wavy hair that fell just above his long eye lashes. His face was kind with just a hint of mischief hidden behind his kind smile. Hunter didn't know a guy could be called beautiful, but he was. It wasn't a girly beautiful, he was just too classically attractive to be called anything else.

"Oh, alright then. In that case let me show where it is.," he said congenially, and Hunter nodded.

"You're going to love it here. It's a good school decent teachers and kick ass sports teams. Do you play any sports?

"Huh, Oh I do kendo." He said truthfully. His father trained him as a child.

"Perfect I'm captain of the Kendo Club. You should come and try-out," he said enthusiastically. Hunter was a bit taken aback by this boy's behavior. Never once has a stranger treated him so kindly. They boy went on about the Kendo Club and Hunter nodded too busy puzzling over him to pay any attention to what he was saying.

"Well here we are," said the boy as Hunter was snapped out of his thoughts.

"Thanks."

"No problem, say what's your name?" said the boy staring directly into his eyes.

"Oh err Hunter," he said as sapphire tried to avoid onyx.

"Hunter eh?" he said tilting his head a bit as he stared. "Cool name. Are you half?"

"Yes."

Ah I see." He said still staring. Hunter felt his face heating up. I think this is the start of an interesting friendship." The boy winked at him then stared down the hall.

"Wait, I didn't get our name!" Hunter called after him. The boy half turned around then he gave a small chuckle.

"Get into the school and then the next time we meet, you'll know my name." He gave Hunter another smile then he continued down the hall waving back to Hunter. "See you around Hunter."

Hunter stared after him thinking 'what a weird guy.' But still this guy intrigued him. Never in his life had he come across someone like him and he was eager to learn about his onyx eyes stranger. When Hunter returned to the office, he was all he could think about.

"Did you find the toilets alright?" Aulia asked

"Err yeah," said Hunter as he sat down beside Liberty.

"Principal Nagashima will see you now," said his secretary and the three of them stood up.

"Please have a seat," said Mr. Nagashima "According to your records you haven't been in school since you were children except for the tutoring you received at the orphanage."

"That is true sir but both of them are extremely bright sir."

"Your parents both attending this academy and the Tachibana remain benefactors. As long as you both pass the entrance exam, I see no reason why you should not allowed to attend Seiryu Academy."

"Thank you sir."

"I'll have my secretary set up a date for you to take the exam."

The exam was set for three days' time. They'd have three days to look over the material. Later that day, the two of them started studying. Hunter could barely pay attention as his thought were interrupted by his onyx eyed stranger. Liberty sensed that he was distracted. She waved her hand in front of his face and then she snapped her fingers.

"Huh what's wrong nee-chan?"

"The questions is what's up with you ni-san? You've been acting weird ever since you came back from the toilet. Did something happen?" she asked suspiciously.

"No, I just ran into this guy," he said in a small voice.

"was he rude to you?" was Liberty's first guess.

"No, just the opposite actually. He was surprisingly nice. Like I looked like just anybody," said Hunter who sounded as surprised as Liberty looked.

"Oh I see," said Liberty strangely annoyed "We haven't been accepted into the school yet and you've already made a friend."

"I wouldn't say he's my friend yet," said Hunter as he looked away from her. He was just really nice to me that's all."

The two continued on studying in silence. Over the next few days up until the day of the exam Hunter and Liberty studied the material. They both passed with flying colors and they were accepted into Seiryu Academy.

The quite life the twins once lived would be over. School would prove to be an intriguing adventure for them. Keeping a low profile will be the least of their worries as an invisible threat creeps around the corner waiting for when they are at their weakest.

Chapter Two - Meet and Greet

HUNTER AND LIBERTY prepared for their first day of school and both were very anxious. However, where Liberty was nervous about being around a lot of people, Hunter was preoccupied with thoughts of his onyx eyed stranger. 'I wonder if I'll even see him today?' he thought to himself as Aulia drove them to school.

"Will you two be okay walking back on your own or shall I arrange for someone to pick you up? I have a couple of errands to run so I don't know when I'll be back," Aulia asked as she stopped in front of the school.

"Don't worry it's not too far," said Liberty "I'll remember."

"Very well. Good luck you two," she said as they exited the car then Aulia drove away. Hunter and Liberty turned to face the school. They didn't realize just how elite Seiryu Academy was until they saw the many limos and fancy cars dropping off students. Some stared as they slowly walked into the school holding hands.

"Be strong." Hunter whispered to Liberty who nodded. Hunter tried to put on a smile as people stared whereas Liberty scowled making many turns away. They entered their homeroom class which went completely silent. The only two empty chairs were in the middle of the room. They sat down just as their teacher entered the room.

"Good morning class."

"Good morning Hirota-sensei."

"We have a pair of new students joining us. Would you two please stand and introduce yourselves."

Hunter stood up first and Liberty reluctantly followed. Hunter was nervous; he wanted to make a good first impression. Liberty knew that her odd appearance would give people an instant impression of her and she did not have the patience to sway them differently.

"My name is Tachibana Hunter

"And I am Tachibana Liberty."

"We are from Hokkaido and we've been home schooled most of our lives," said Hunter telling them a lie.

"What activities do you enjoy?" Hirota-sensei asked

"Err I like to practice Kendo and martial arts," said Hunter saying the first thing that came to his mind. He nudged Liberty.

"I enjoy reading and playing the violin," she said which wasn't a complete lie. Liberty had been playing the violin since she was a child.

"Thank you very much for introducing yourselves you may be seated."

Hunter released a sigh of relief as he sat down feeling like the worst was over. People whispered around them as Hirota-sensei went over the day's lesson. In the middle of class, a student walked in.

"Sorry to disturb the class sensei but President Takahashi has an announcement he wants me to make on behalf of the student council," said the boy

"Please proceed," said Hirota-sensei

The boy nodded then walked to the top of the classroom holding up a piece of paper.

"To my fellow Third years as you know, we have tragically lost our Vice President to a different school so we are in need of a new one. Since we cannot have a proper election in the middle of term, any student who think they have what it takes to be the Vice President please see me. I will interview people for the position and the best qualified candidate will be announced at the end of the month. Needless to say, all candidates must have excellent grades. Can't wait to see who will try for the position.

Good luck.

That is all." The boy bowed then left. The room erupted into excited chatter.

"In wonder who's going to try?"

"This is the first time anything like this has happened."

"Trust King Taka to make something as simple choosing a Vice President into a contest of who can impress him the most."

"Is the school really going to allow such a thing?"

"Of course he's King Taka."

"Excuse me class but this is neither the time nor the place to be discussing this," said Hirota-sensei loudly and the classroom went silent.

"That's a very odd way to pick a Vice President," Hunter whispered to liberty

"You mean stupid," she replied.

As soon as class was over the chattering started all over again. Hunter was vaguely interested in this person they all 'King Taka' whereas Liberty tried to ignore them.

She was grateful that they were now too distracted to stare at her. Except for one boy in particular who could not keep his eyes off her. However, he did not look scared or put off by her. In fact, he looked rather intrigued. Liberty could not his face clearly, but his eyes shown out clearly. Liberty had never seen such stunning green eyes before. His hair was dirty blond and spiked. He wore a few earrings on his ear and a choker around his neck. Suddenly the boy turned to face her directly and started daringly into her eyes. Liberty could almost feel his eyes taking in every inch of her body. She felt uncomfortable under his gaze and quickly turned away from him. She regained her composure and looked cautiously over her shoulder only to find that the boy was gone. She looked around the classroom, but he was nowhere in sight. Liberty sat pondering what just happened completely ignoring the commotion around her.

Hunter was too busy listening to the conversations to notice Liberty's discomfort.

"Are you going to try to be the next Vice President Tanaka?"

"You'd be a shoe in Tanaka, you ran in the last election and you only lost by a small number of votes."

"Yes it seems only natural that I get the position," said one boy pompously. "I don't see why President Takahashi is even considering anyone else I am the obvious choice and one is stupid enough to go against me."

"King Taka must obviously think there is someone better for the job or he would not be doing this in the first place Tanaka."

"You people are being played by that pretty boy Takahashi. The sooner I get on the student council the sooner I knock that fake king off his thrown."

"You wish Tanaka."

This 'Kin Taka' obviously had a lot of power over the students and the class was split with some of them rallying for Tanaka and the most behind Takahashi for a different Vice-President.

By the end of their next class Hunter found out more about the person they called 'King Taka'. He apparently ran unchallenged for the class Presidency race, since the other two candidates dropped out halfway through.

About the Author

Vivienne St. Louis is a writer, lyricist, and a teacher.

She has been writing and collecting her work since she was 13 years old.

Now she lives in Japan where she teaches English as a Second Language.

Vivienne enjoys playing tennis, figure skating, dancing, K-Pop, and video games.

1

vivisaint.weebly.com

1. https://d.docs.live.net/19ee8bc3bf2eba56/Documents/

Image%20by%20%3ca%20href=%22https:/pixabay.com/users/

Clker-Free-Vector-Images-3736/?utm_source=link-attribution&utm_medium=referral&a

mp;utm_campaign=image&utm_content=42414%22%3eClker-Free-Vector-Images%3c/

a%3e%20from%20%3ca%20href=%22https://pixabay.com/?utm_source=link-attribution&am

p;utm_medium=referral&utm_campaign=image&utm_content=42414%22%3ePixa

bay%3c/a%3e

Don't miss out!

Visit the website below and you can sign up to receive emails whenever Vivienne Saint Louis publishes a new book. There's no charge and no obligation.

https://books2read.com/r/B-A-MFRJ-CLOKB

BOOKS 2 READ

Connecting independent readers to independent writers.

Did you love *Faith Spiritwolfe - Aria Towards Destruction*? Then you should read *Dreaming Awake - Selected Poetry and Prose*[2] by Vivienne Saint Louis!

Deep dive into this imaginative collection of **poetry** and **prose**. A world of thoughts and dreams carefully constructed into four distinct parts filled with science fiction, fantasy, romance, and nature illustrating life from adolescence to adulthood. **Dreaming Awake** takes you on a journey through the author's mind with dark and captivating prose poems, rhythmic lyrics, free verse poems, and daily musings. Examining life and the struggles and jubilations that fill it, tackling issues like loss, depression, love, suicide, sexual abuse, anxiety, and self-discovery.

---

2. https://books2read.com/u/bOxVnE

3. https://books2read.com/u/bOxVnE

A perfect companion for a long journey or a short coffee break. It's an audiobook you can pick and listen to a different poem each time. If poems about real life appeal to you, then Dreaming Awake is right for you.

Read more at https://www.vivisaint.weebly.com.

Also by Vivienne Saint Louis

The Sister's Affinity
Faith Spiritwolfe Pain and Knowledge
Faith Spiritwolfe - Aria Towards Destruction

Standalone
Dreaming Awake - Selected Poetry and Prose

Watch for more at https://www.vivisaint.weebly.com.